the
hour
between

the hour between

A NOVEL

Sebastian Stuart

ALYSON*books*

The Hour Between

Published by Alyson Books
245 West 17th Street, Suite 1200, New York, NY 10011
www.alyson.com

Library of Congress Cataloging-in-Publication data is on file.

ISBN-10: 1-59350-126-9
ISBN-13: 978-1-59350-126-6

10 9 8 7 6 5 4 3 2 1

Cover design by Michael Fusco
Book interior by Maria E. Torres, Neuwirth & Associates, Inc.

Printed in the United States of America
Distributed by Consortium Book Sales and Distribution
Distribution in the United Kingdom by Turnaround Publisher Services Ltd.

For Stephen McCauley,
and all the hours after

the
hour
between

Prologue

THE PLACES I have lived—a neighborhood, a house, a landscape—
retain a deep hold on me, no matter how many years go by. There
is, for example, the campus in the Connecticut countryside where I
spent my senior year of high school. The property had been an inn at
one time and was dotted with rustic cabins, a rambling main house,
and a little lake with an island in the middle, on which a weeping willow hung its mournful branches. The buildings were in need
of paint, the shrubs were untended, the pine-paneled rooms were
damp and creaky, and the whole place had that chill melancholy air
that one associates with New England in the autumn. Still, I loved
my year there—it was my first time away from home and family, the
place where I made my first real friends, where I took my first steps
toward the independence I yearned for.

That was all a long time ago, and the children who were my
friends back then are scattered who knows where. Katrina Felt was
the most important to me, but in recent years even she crossed my
mind only now and then. That is until I got that breathless call from
Jeffrey Wilcox.

Jeffrey had also been a schoolmate, and although now we both
lived in San Francisco, we saw each other rarely, crossing paths on
the street or at this or that party. Jeffrey had done well, was some
mucky-muck at a bank downtown; he and his partner lived in the

perfect Victorian above the Castro and were obsessed with Gilbert and Sullivan, group sex, and their dachshunds. (I lived in a rambling old flat in the Mission, made a tolerable living as a freelance writer, and enjoyed movies, long bike rides through Golden Gate Park, and a twenty-year semi-open relationship with a man who shall remain nameless.) It was only recently that Jeffrey, tight on mojitos at some dreary windswept barbeque, had confessed to me that he had shared my fixation with Katrina during that long-ago year, had in fact been jealous of my intimacy with her. I wasn't surprised—it was fearsome easy to fall in love with Katrina Felt.

So when Jeffrey called me, late last Thursday afternoon, I knew immediately that it had to be about Katrina.

"Arthur, I'm at the airport, just got off a flight from Edinburgh, can I come over, I have something you have *got* to see."

As I waited for Jeffrey to show up, I made blueberry muffins and a pot of Darjeeling, spiked with a bit of cognac, as much to welcome Jeffrey as to calm my own anticipation of what his news of Katrina might be. For a luscious little while I allowed myself to imagine that they would climb out of the taxi together, that she had been on his flight, they had reconnected, stories spilling out, and that when she had learned that I lived in San Francisco, she had *insisted* on *dashing* right over. But when Jeffrey walked up the staircase to my flat, he was alone.

Jeffrey, dressed in a suit as always, had been an effeminate, bone-skinny boy and was a bone-skinny man, with a long thin head and a milky spot in one pupil that I'd always found touching; his effeminacy had aged into a distinguished rectitude. He dropped his suitcase and walked right past me, down the long hallway into my front parlor. I followed. He sat on my sofa.

"Something amazing happened in Edinburgh."

"You ran into Katrina."

"In a manner of speaking, yes."

"What manner?"

"Sit," Jeffrey said, indicating the spot beside him; I obeyed. "I was over there for a conference, which had just finished. I had an hour to kill before the orgy started and I decided to do a little gallery hopping. Well, I happened to come upon a gallery with *this* picture in the window." He reached into his briefcase and pulled out a large manila envelope, from which he withdrew a thin catalogue. The painting on the cover was striking, of a woman perched on the edge of an enormous red brocade divan, a small-boned woman with a helmet of shiny black hair, huge dark eyes, and a full mouth with the slightest overbite; she was wearing a slim cool black dress, had one leg curved under her, a tiny monkey perched on her left shoulder; she looked straight out from the canvas, pulling me in, pulling me back to that year, with a gaze that was pure Katrina: playful, soulful, seductive, wistful. But the years had brought, as the years do, more to her face, to her eyes, and this Katrina met the world with the weary rueful sympathy that defines for me great French actresses of a certain age.

"It's her," Jeffrey said.

"It certainly is." I looked at the artist's name: Taziz Erbani.

"I went in, of course. Erbani is apparently quite famous in Turkey. I asked the gallery owner if he knew anything about the woman in the painting and he showed me the artist's statement."

"Did you get a copy?"

"Yes, dear, I got a copy. Calm down." Jeffrey took out a roll of Life Savers and slowly peeled out a candy, which he placed in his mouth with his peculiar precision. Then he pulled a piece of paper from the envelope and handed it to me. I read:

"This woman is my inspiration for she makes me laugh and feel alive and when I hold her I feel I am holding mercury. We are a secret couple for she is married to a big man of Istanbul and has three children and even a granddaughter. She gives parties in her palace on the Bosporus that are magical and if you are very lucky she will sing and you will cry."

I looked from the words to the image, to Katrina.

"The gallery owner told me Erbani sent the painting to Edinburgh because he couldn't show it in Istanbul, there would be a scandal. You look stunned, Arthur. And you also need a shave."

Jeffrey left and I went to the bedroom and retrieved an old photo album from the back of a closet. Its cover was ratty and its pages yellowed, but the pictures I'd taken of the campus were still there: the main house, the tiny lake, the sagging cabins, and there, alone on its own page, mossy and vine-crept, was the stone wall where I had first caught sight of Katrina Felt.

1

IT WAS EARLY September 1967. I'd just been kicked out of Collegiate, which is in Manhattan and claims to be the oldest boys' school in the country, and my folks were driving me up to Connecticut to enroll me in a boarding school known for being liberal, artsy, and, most crucial, for having a fast and lenient admissions policy. I felt guilty putting them through this but I just couldn't face another year at Collegiate—strangling ties and that itchy wool blazer, chapel and Latin and sports. So I didn't go. I'd leave the house in the morning and walk down to the Donnell Library Center on West Fifty-third Street, where I'd look at picture books about Hollywood and the movies until it was time to go home. I got the idea from a production of *The Glass Menagerie* I'd seen in London the summer before. My Laura phase lasted the

first week of school and gave Collegiate the excuse it was looking for to give me the boot.

After getting off some turnpike or other, we drove along pleasant
country roads for a while until we came to a battered wooden sign:
THE SPOONER SCHOOL. We turned down a long oak-lined drive. On
one side was the small lake with its island and weeping willow, on the
other side a field bordered by that old stone wall. And there she was
atop the wall, Katrina Felt, her arms held out for balance, moving
quickly, almost recklessly, but with such grace and buoyancy that I
craned my head to watch: would *she* be one of my classmates?

We came to the school's main building, a rambling old pile sprouting porches, gables, turrets; across a stretch of flagstone sat an empty
swimming pool, its cracked concrete faded a delicate pastel blue;
the boys' dorm was across a green; little cabins dotted the grounds;
the girls' dorm, a modern split-level house, sat atop a small hill.
The whole campus was neglected—paint peeling, hedges sprouting
shooters, roofs home to tiny hills of moss—in a way that I found
charming and romantic.

"Well, here we are." Mom turned and gave me a strained smile.
"They're terribly keen on the arts, it's going to be smashing." Mom
grew up in London in a family of scholars and academics and even
after decades in the States held fast to her Deborah Kerr–ness.

As we got out of the car, a small bird-like woman in clunky black
shoes clipped out of the main house and crossed the gravel with
an excited step, her bobbed gray hair flapping at the sides of her
head like wings, her tiny gray eyes alight. "Welcome to the Spooner
School!" Her accent was English, as was her cheery avian smile, the
tight little mouth darting up on either side of the small beak. She
stuck out an arm, rigid at the elbow, in my direction, "I'm Miss
Wimple, and you must be Arthur."

"It's nice to meet you," I said.

"Hello, Mr. and Mrs. MacDougal. He's in good hands."

"We've no doubt," Mom said, laying on the accent thick as marmalade. The two beamed at each other in a fit of Anglo bonding.

"Would you like a quick tour? We're busy as mad bees, of course. Semester starts on the morrow, bright and early."

"We have a dinner," Mom said. "But we'll be back up."

Dad shook my hand, Mom kissed me.

"Thanks, and I'm sorry," I said.

They smiled, then got in the car and drove off, lighting cigarettes.

"After you meet Mr. Spooner, I'll show you to your room," Miss Wimple said. A phone rang from inside the house. "Oh goodness! I feel like a piece of taffy! I'll be right back, dear boy. *Com-ing!*" she yelled to the phone as she sped away.

I looked toward the field and saw Katrina, now sitting cross-legged on the wall. I raised my arm in an awkward wave. She smiled, jumped down, and started toward me. She was small and had a springy step. I sat on the front stoop and tried not to look too nervous.

"Do you like my Gidget Goes to Paris look?" she asked when she was in front of me. Then she twirled around and struck a pose, fists on hips. She was wearing black capri pants, white sneakers, and a black-and-white-striped boat-neck top. Her black hair was short and spiky; her enormous round dark eyes, lined in black; her nose, slightly upturned; her lips, with that faint overbite, lipsticked in a lush red. Equal parts elf, urchin, enfant terrible, she was the most adorable thing I'd ever clapped eyes on.

"*Oui,*" I said.

She sat down beside me and pulled up her knees. "Oh, thank God, I wasn't sure what was apropos for a tony New England boarding school. Although I'm not sure how tony this dive is. Isn't it divinely

dilapidated? I wonder if Mumsie read the catalogue wrong. My last
lycee was in Switzerland and it looked like a mountain resort. I could
hardly stop myself from yodeling between classes. Cig?" She pulled
out a silver cigarette case and matching lighter and snapped the case
open. "Dunhills, got hooked on them one mad weekend in Sussex.
Or was it Essex? Anyway, there was sex in it, wherever it was. *A lot
of sex.*" She tilted the case in my direction.

"I don't smoke."

"No one's perfect." She lit up, inhaled, and blew out the smoke
in a faux grown-up way, as if she was infinitely weary. "By the way,
name's Katrina. You can call me Kat, but I'd rather you didn't."

"I'm Arthur."

"*C'est mon plaisir.*"

"Where are you from, Katrina?"

"Oh God, *that* question. I'm a nomad, tromping from oasis to
oasis. And this is my latest watering hole. Mostly L.A. A bit of
London. Rome sometimes. I was in L.A. all summer, got in a spot
of trouble, I did. That's why I got shipped off to sturdy, solid old
New England, to turn me into a Norman Rockwell girl."

"Trouble?"

"Oh, it was nothing," she said, a little too dismissively. She took a
deep pull on her cigarette. "If you must know, the powers-that-be felt
that I was involved with an inappropriate boy. I learned an important
lesson: that one must move on-on-*on*. End of story, okay? And where
are you from, Arthur?"

"New York."

"Mumsie's just taken a place at the Sherry-Netherland. I think she's
going to do a play. Sad. She hates theater. But the movie offers aren't
exactly flooding in these days. Poor Mumsie," she said, and her face
darkened. She raked her fingers through her hair and shook her head

in a gesture I would come to know well, one that signaled a quick turn away from terrain she found foreboding. "Just to get it out of the way, I should probably tell you that my mother is Jean Clarke."

"The movie star?"

"No, darling, the cleaning lady. Yes, the movie star. Silly boy." She stood up and spun around, taking in the campus. "Can you imagine? Me in New England. Will I have to learn manners and all that? How proper. Shall we call Kate Hepburn? Mom hates her—professional jealousy, don'cha know."

Jean Clarke's daughter! Jean Clarke was *so* fabulous, not the world's most beautiful movie star, but what style and verve, you couldn't take your eyes off her. I wanted to ask Katrina a million questions about her mom, but thought it might be rude, not to mention pathetically star-struck and gushy.

"Don't tell me—you *adore* her. All fairies—no wait, *gay* is the new word, Laurence Harvey told me, over drinks in the Polo Lounge. Anyway, all gay boys adore Mummy. You should see them at parties and openings; it's moths to a flame."

Just like that, tossing it off, she'd pegged me for . . . gay. I mean, I knew I was no John Wayne, but was it *that* obvious? Before I had time to recover, Miss Wimple burst out the front door.

"I spoke with Mr. Spooner, he'll see the two of you together, come along now, chop-chop."

⌒〜

MISS WIMPLE KNOCKED on the closed door: "Katrina Felt and Arthur MacDougal are here, Mr. Spooner." We were on the second-floor landing, dulcet piano tones drifted down the hall, and as we waited for a response, my anxiety grew—headmasters came right after crazed ax murderers on my People-to-Avoid list. Katrina gave my hand a quick squeeze. I was glad she was around to divert attention from me.

The door opened, slowly, silently, and there stood Mr. Spooner, looking at us with bright blue eyes. Miss Wimple disappeared, and we followed him into the large room; an Oriental rug, bookcases, a few chairs, and an oak desk dotted the expanse. Mr. Spooner turned toward a bank of windows, hands clasped behind his back. A bead of sweat rolled down from my armpit. Katrina gave me a playful look and I marveled at her nonchalance.

"It's a lovely day," he said.

The windows opened up onto the sky, the lake, the last green of summer.

"It's a *divine* day, Mr. Spooner, makes one want to write poetry or fall in love or get drunk, or perhaps all three," Katrina said, blithely pulling out her cigarette case and lighting up.

Mr. Spooner turned, shot a glance at the cigarette but said nothing, and began to pace the length of the room, head down, thoughtful. He was wearing gray flannel slacks and a navy cardigan, had a sharp, smooth face with a wide forehead, a pointed chin, a tight mouth, and those clear knowing eyes—all in all he was striking but not sexy, like one of those cold English movie stars. He turned and looked at us. I tried a smile but it came out closer to a twitch.

"We're so glad you're both here," he said, sitting behind his desk, erect yet relaxed; with a tiny nod he indicated the two chairs across from him.

"Thank you, Mr. Spooner. I'm glad to be here," I said.

"Ditto, darling," Katrina said, sitting down and flicking her ash into a small silver bowl that didn't look like an ashtray to me. And had she just called the headmaster "darling"?

"You both wrote excellent essays."

We'd been required to write two pages (double spaced) on "What I Hope to Find at the Spooner School." Since I was in a guilt-ridden panic when I wrote the essay and what I hoped to find was a school that would accept me, I'd written about my hope to be part of a learning community that would enable me to grow as a human being. Or something along those lines.

"I just rambled, because the truth is I haven't a clue what I hope to find here, and I don't *want* to know, in fact if some genie popped out of a magic lamp and said, 'Abracadabra, Katrina baby, I have come to tell you what you'll find at the Spooner School,' I'd say, 'Oh, shut up, you silly genie, and hightail it right back into that magic lamp,' because if I knew, why then all the mystery would be gone, all the surprise, all the *pow!* and all the *wow!*"

Mr. Spooner smiled, "What you lacked in specificity you made up for in style. And your essay, Arthur, showed a certain spiritual yearning, a sense of wonder." I wondered if he'd gotten mine mixed up with someone else's. "We encourage that here at the Spooner School. Education should be a glorious thing, and so often it isn't. Rules, restraints, confines—they don't really work, do they? You can't shove knowledge down a child as if he were a foie-gras goose. No, true learning comes when a hungry mind devours knowledge." He stood up, his voice rising with passion. "I want my school to make its students ravenous—culture, history, the natural world, language, art, poetry, the great sweeping saga of mankind! What a feast!"

"Pass the ketchup and let's chow down!" Katrina cried, while I stared at the bulging vein in Mr. Spooner's forehead.

Like *that* he regained his composure, and calmly lifted a crusty black rock off his desk. "This is a piece of the Zarata meteorite. It fell to earth in a suburb of Buenos Aires in 1903: six hundred tons,

three hundred feet across, four stories tall. The Indians thought it
was a tear from the eye of the moon god, so they tried to keep the
scientists away from it. There was a massacre. The scientists got their
meteorite. But not before the Indians had put a curse on it—"

"Oh, yummy fun, what kind of curse?" Katrina asked, leaning
forward and taking an intense pull on her cigarette.

"Ah, I've whet your appetite," Mr. Spooner said. He put the rock
back on the desk. "We'll save that meal for another time. I'm sure
you both want to get settled."

~

OUT IN THE hallway, Katrina leaned into me and whispered, "*Quel
planet is he from?*"

"He is intense, isn't he?"

"He reminds me of Tony Perkins. You do *not* want to find yourself
alone with Tony in someone's pool house at three in the morning.
Especially if you're a boy. Although Spooner did make me want to
crack a book, or visit a museum, or do *something* bettering."

Just then a door opened behind us.

"Isn't Mr. Spooner the most extraordinary man?" Miss Wimple
sighed. Behind her was a room run riot with lace and doilies. A huge
shapeless figure, in a flowered Victorian dress and topped with an
exuberant halo of white hair, sat playing an upright piano. "Come
meet Miss McCoy."

Katrina and I followed Miss Wimple into the room, which had
floral wallpaper—bright bursting peonies—and candy dishes everywhere, filled with multicolored gumdrops and jellybeans. The place
was almost sticky with a sweet spiritual warmth. Miss McCoy was
ancient, with a large fleshy face that jiggled; she beamed at us from

behind her wire-rimmed glasses, playing gently, a hymn, *Shall We Gather by the River*.

"Miss McCoy, this is Katrina Felt and Arthur MacDougal."

Miss McCoy went on playing, lost in her sugary bliss. "Miss McCoy is our music teacher."

"Nice to meet you," I said.

"*Enchanté,*" Katrina said.

Miss McCoy's expression didn't change. Was the music teacher deaf?

The hymn swelled and Miss Wimple swooned, her eyes glazed like donuts. Then Katrina closed her eyes and began to hum along. I can't carry a tune in a suitcase but I knew perfect pitch when I heard it, and her humming had a soulful quality that pulled me right into the music, stirring and sad, and gave me goosebumps.

When the hymn ended Miss Wimple turned to her, "*Well done,* young lady, you have a lovely tone." Katrina glowed.

Then Miss McCoy looked at us as if for the first time. "WHO'S THIS?" she screamed.

"This is Katrina Felt and Arthur MacDougal, Miss McCoy. They're two of this year's new students."

Miss McCoy's huge white face dissolved into a smile; her teeth were tiny yellow nubs. She reached up and grabbed a fistful of gumdrops from a dish on top of the piano and shoveled several into her mouth. "Gumdrops," she announced.

"Miss McCoy does love her gumdrops and jellybeans. Makes Christmas shopping such a lesser trial," Miss Wimple said.

"WHAT?!" Miss McCoy screamed.

"CHRISTMAS, MISS MCCOY, CHRISTMAS!" Miss Wimple screamed back.

"NO FUDGE!"

"She has digestive problems. Lactose. Tends to be gaseous," Miss Wimple explained.

As if on cue, Miss McCoy broke bold wind. Katrina giggled.

"Good-bye, dear, the music was so lovely," Miss Wimple said, giving my arm a firm tug.

"NO FUDGE!" Miss McCoy screamed after us.

As we left, Katrina tapped my shoulder and pointed to a book sitting prominently on a small round reading table—*Science and Health with Key to the Scriptures,* by Mary Baker Eddy.

"She must be a Christian Scientist," she whispered. "L.A. is thick with them. They're *très* bizarre—they have a secret smile and their eyes glow."

⁓

"HERE YOU ARE then," Miss Wimple said, after pulling me away from Katrina and leading me up to my room in the boys' dorm. "I'm not quite sure who your roommate will be." It looked like a rustic inn from one of those comfy old Bing Crosby movies—knotty pine wainscoting, two knotty pine beds and dressers, and a private bath; an oak desk was the only clue this was a school. The building creaked a little and smelled like wood, cold, and New England. "Oh, I do think you're going to like it here at the Spooner School, Arthur," she said, and with one last twinkle, she left.

I was alone in the hollow building. I lay on the bed by the window—the brown wool blanket smelled faintly of mothballs—and looked out at the campus. I could see Katrina down by the lake. She picked up a stone and skimmed it across the surface; it skipped a half-dozen times and she jumped up and down in exaggerated celebration, as if she knew she was being watched.

I was still in shock over her gay comment; after all, my sexuality was the defining crisis of my neurotic young life. Not only was it about sex and love and that whole trauma, and telling people you were gay and *that* whole trauma, there was the matter of my appearance to make peace with. Gay boys should be beautiful and soulful, like that boy in *Death in Venice,* or Montgomery Clift. I, on the other hand, was blander than white bread—with my neatly parted hair and ordinary features I looked like a throwback to the fifties, squaresville, a poster boy for the Young Republicans. And I'd shot up to six feet in about two weeks; no matter what sleeve or pants length I wore, my bony wrists and ankles escaped, announcing to the world that I was a dork. A gay dork. And until a half hour earlier, no one had known my secret.

But mixed up with my shock was an immense sense of relief; I felt lighter, as if I was suddenly breathing freely, getting more oxygen. Katrina had made it so easy for me—it was over just like that, no big deal. I looked out at her again: a large frog sat in the palm of her hand, she was gently petting it and telling it something that looked terribly important. I wanted to be with her, to hear what she saying to that lucky frog.

"We're roommates, Arthur MacDougal, I requested you." I turned and saw a boy about my age. He plopped on the other bed, lit a cigarette, inhaled, and opened his mouth—a thick stream of smoke poured out and up his nose in a reverse waterfall. "When I heard a rumor you'd been kicked out of Collegiate, I knew you couldn't be all bad. Nicholas Meyers. Pleasure."

Nicholas was great looking, thin, with thick black hair, fierce dark eyes, a full devilish mouth, a large rugged nose. And he was my roommate. God, I hadn't had a roommate since that summer camp in Maine when I was ten, and that only lasted four nights, two of them bed-wetted, before I stopped eating and Dad had to come and get me.

"Spooner's a great place. Edward Spooner is the original space cadet. He's a Christian Scientist, they all are, his inner sanctum," Nicholas continued. "But this isn't a Christian Science school per se, it just sort of floats around the edges. In other words, if you slit your wrists they *will* take you to the emergency room. My father founded Meyers Press. We hate each other. My mother killed herself. My father pretends to be a liberal. But he isn't." He smashed his cigarette out in a small metal ashtray. "It's all right, though, he'll die. Let's go for a walk."

WE WENT OUT behind the main building, where the land sloped down to the lake, and sat on the grass. The sky was a pale cloudless blue, a family of ducks glided across the water, the chicks safe inside the spreading V of their mother's wake.

"I'm bored already," Katrina said, appearing from around the other side of the building. "The problem with the country is all the trees. They're *everywhere*. Your emotions bounce off of them and come back at you in waves. It's *très* disconcerting." She lay down and slung one leg over the other, the upper leg bouncing, restless.

"Stick around, sister, you won't be bored for long," Nicholas said.

"Says who?"

"Katrina, this is Nicholas."

"I love that name, it's got bite and melody: *Nicholas*—Saint Nicholas, Czar Nicholas, *our* Nicholas."

"I'll try not to disappoint."

Just then a girl came roaring down the hill like a bear: large, not very coordinated, and pray she doesn't have to stop on a dime. "Nicky!"

Nicholas's face lit up and he ran to her. "Sapphire!"

They met in a running hug that turned round and round, then they pulled apart, looked at each other, jumped up and down.

"Nicky! Fuck face!"

"Sapphire! Slut from hell!"

They fell to the grass laughing, laughing. I felt left out; Katrina lit a cigarette.

"Your summer?" Sapphire asked when they'd finally cooled down.

"Long and hot and humid, East Hampton is the world's poshest swamp. Yours?"

"Totally incredible. Went white-water rafting on mescaline, spent a week in a cave at the bottom of the Grand Canyon, balled identical twins."

Nicholas looked hurt for a second and then quickly recovered with, "At the same time?"

"Yes. I was pretty stoned, kept thinking I was seeing double."

"It's the dawning of the Age of Aquarius, *not* the Age of Gemini."

"Well, *they* were Aquarius."

"Sapphire."

"Nicky."

They rolled over on their backs and looked at the sky with goofy smiles, then Sapphire cocked an eye over at me and Katrina. "Who're they?" She had a great round face, still flush with baby fat, the brown eyes twinkled with good humor, the nose was a squashed button, the mouth a loose wavy slash. Her thick curly brown hair was flying every which way, and her plump body was swaddled in an Indian wraparound skirt and a Mexican peasant blouse; she was barefoot.

"That's Arthur. He was kicked out of Collegiate."

"Congratulations."

"And Katrina comes to us from Los Angeles."

"Groovy. Let's get high," Sapphire said with a big grin, reaching down into her panties and pulling out a joint.

⁓

AT THE FAR end of the campus there was a path leading into the woods; we were on it. I found woods eerie, lonely; I'd ride the IRT at midnight, but when my folks dragged me up to friends' places in Roxbury or Litchfield I'd set out on long walks, end up spooked after fifty feet, slink back to the house, find an out-of-the-way den, turn on the TV, and watch an old movie. But being with Nicholas, Sapphire, and Katrina I felt protected—I mean, once you get past the terror, woods are pretty places.

"The Spot!" Sapphire cried. She ran ahead to a small clearing: the ground was covered with pine needles and there was a sooty rock-pile hearth with a couple of log benches. She started to skip around like a demented wood nymph.

"I love Sapphire," Nicholas said in a voice tinged with melancholy.

Sapphire stopped in front of Katrina and me. She looked like a witch with her exploding hair and Frisbee eyes. "Close your eyes," she ordered. We did. She came close, smelling like patchouli oil, warm female musk, and cheap Indian cotton. She kissed our foreheads, took our hands, and led us forward. "*Open*—the Spot welcomes Arthur and Katrina," she said in this light/heavy way that reminded me of a Joni Mitchell song.

"Hi, Spot," Katrina said.

We all sat in a circle and they lit the joint. I didn't want to admit that I'd only smoked pot once before, at my cousin's wedding on Martha's Vineyard. A bunch of us had gotten stoned at the reception, which was held at a beach club, and I'd immediately had a massive paranoia attack, sure that everyone could tell I was stoned. I went and curled into a little ball on the back seat of my parents' car; when I finally reappeared my cousins asked me where I'd been and I told them I'd been down by the ocean communing with the surf. They thought that was cool. But I knew I had to learn to smoke pot, so I took a hit and immediately went into a coughing fit, waved off any more, and struggled to regain my dignity.

"Let's be roommates," Sapphire said to Katrina.

"Let's. We'll do a hippie-dippy thing, all milk crates, peacock feathers, and the *I Ching*."

"Have you met our so-called dorm mother, Mrs. Markum?"

"Rhinestone glasses, a poodle pin, and booze blasting off her breath? Yes."

"Avoid her at all costs in the morning. At night she's usually passed out by eight thirty, so it's a cinch to sneak out. Poor Mrs. Markum, it's not easy being a chain-smoking alcoholic in a den of Christian Scientists," Sapphire said.

"It's not easy being a fucked-up teenager in a den of Christian Scientists, either," Nicholas said.

Sapphire rumpled his hair, "Yes, it is."

"Oh, Sapphire," Nicholas said in exasperated delight.

"I do like it here—it's of-the-earth earthy, pagan and primitive," Katrina said, looking around.

"Hey, Nicky, I like these two," Sapphire said, cocking her head toward me and Katrina.

"They're okay," Nicholas agreed.

Sapphire leaned in toward us, "Let's us four make a pact to be best friends this year."

"Oh let's, the Four Mouseketeers! We'll fight hypocrisy, boredom, and homework," Katrina said.

Nicholas stuck out a hand, "One for all." We piled our hands on top of his until we had an eight-layered sandwich. "And all for one!" we cried.

I felt a surge of exhilaration—I couldn't believe I was actually being accepted, even offered friendship. I'd been pretty much a loner at Collegiate. In fact, I hadn't had a real friend since Peter Fisher in third grade, and he'd dropped me after I suggested we dress up in his mother's clothes.

I took another hit of pot and managed to hold it down. The sky was darkening and the woods seemed to close in around us, the air was soft, twilight was here, and the world seemed far away.

Katrina leaned her head on my shoulder and I suddenly felt protective of her; in a low intimate voice she said, "I love this time of day, Arthur. The French call it the hour between the dog and the wolf."

The wind lifted a nearby leaf; a shiver ran up my spine.

⁓

DINNER WAS SERVED in the main house, in a homey pine-paneled room with a fireplace. Nicholas, Sapphire, Katrina, and I sat together. Spooner's boarding contingent, about twenty in all, had trickled in during the day and were scattered around the room. There was a table of upper-middle-class types, the girls with long straight hair and dangly earrings, the boys with tweed sports coats and tousled hair—very Nantucket, very Volvo. At another table I saw Jeffrey Wilcox for the first time—thin and pimply, with that touching milky spot in his left pupil. He was sitting with several other nerdy-looking kids. At Collegiate, that would have been my table, the geek table. I felt guilty about abandoning my people, but not guilty enough to join them.

"I always have a cocktail with dinner, so civilized," Katrina said, taking a silver flask out of her purse. "*Un peu de* gin, anyone?" Nicholas and I demurred, but she and Sapphire spiked their apple juice. Katrina took a long sip, shivered with delight, and said, "We've invented a new drink. Let's call it the Spooner."

"Booze is so passé. Have you tried LSD?" Nicholas asked her.

"*Mais oui.*"

He turned to me. I shook my head.

"Did you ever go to the supermarket tripping? The colors!" Sapphire said.

"I flew to Paris tripping," Nicholas bragged.

"I had dinner at the Brown Derby with Audrey Hepburn tripping," Katrina tossed off.

"Katrina Go-stoned-ly," Nicholas managed.

"What was Audrey Hepburn like on LSD?" I asked.

"Thin."

Drugs scared me—of course, so did just about everything else—but part of me wanted to feel like I was part of the whole hippie movement. I admired their anti-establishment philosophy, but I had a hard time getting past the tie-dye clothes, swirly posters, and all that grungy facial hair; plus, incense made me nauseous.

"I'd love to ball Martin Luther King," Sapphire said in a neat segue.

"Undeniably a great man," Nicholas said.

"I love his color—that dusky black—and he's so *soul*ful, not in a soul music way, but in a way that makes you feel sad and wise and filled with love," Katrina said.

"Let's write him a letter!" Sapphire exclaimed.

Nicholas found a pen, but none of us had paper, so Sapphire opened her napkin.

"Dear Dr. King, we shall overcome. All my best, Nicholas Meyers."

"Dear Martin, we think you are a great man and your wife is a lucky woman. If you're ever in Westridge, Connecticut, visit the girls' dorm. Love, Sapphire."

"Dear Dr. King, I share your dream, Arthur MacDougal."

"Darling Martin, My housekeeper Ethel has your picture in her bedroom and we watched your speech at the March on Washington together and cried and cried. *Bon courage*, Your Katrina."

Sapphire carefully refolded the napkin. "I'll mail it tomorrow."

Katrina refreshed her drink and said, looking around, "This room gives me a terrible case of the ughs. The wood paneling reminds me of some TV actor's rec room, all that's missing is the bar and the dartboard. Let's paint it over—we'll make it an art project. After all, we're here to fight hypocrisy, boredom, and dreary rooms. Dreary shrivels the soul. Come on, Mouseketeers."

And with that we all followed her down to the art studio, which was in the basement next to the "theater department." We put on blue smocks and under Katrina's direction mixed up a gingery orange color that managed to be both cheerful and sophisticated.

"It's divine, just looking at it jazzes me up. We'll call it . . . Abba-Dabba! Tomorrow we'll go into town and buy five gallons. There *is* a town somewhere out here, isn't there?"

⌒

TEETH AND FACE scrubbed for bed, I walked out of the bathroom
to find a very large man standing in our doorway, a warm gruff
smile on his face. "Evening, gentlemen, I'm Mr. Tupper."

"Hello," I said.

Nicholas, lying on his bed reading *Naked Lunch*, gave a little grunt.

Mr. Tupper was burly, about fifty, with thick white hair, a ruddy
face, friendly blue eyes, and a long white beard; in overalls and a
plaid shirt, he was equal parts Ann Arbor and Santa's workshop.
"Mrs. Tupper and I live down at the end of the hall, we're your
dorm parents. I also teach English and History, and I'm the assistant
headmaster. As far as dorm rules go, we're all grown-ups here, so
common sense prevails. After all, this is 1967." Then he laughed
in that pathetic way grown-ups do when they want to be liked and
thought "with it."

He had an arm propped up against the doorjamb—suddenly a
pudgy porcine face popped under it. "Hi, boys!"

"This is Nicholas and Arthur, mother."

I'd never heard a grown man call his wife "mother" before.

"I'm Joan, but you can call me mom or mother, just don't call
me late for dinner."

I laughed, Nicholas didn't—I knew I could take a leisurely walk
from here to eternity before I'd hear him call her "mom." With her
round pink face and upturned nose, I couldn't help thinking that she
looked like Porky Pig. Santa and Porky stood there beaming at us.

"It's a pleasure to meet you," I said.

"Howdoyoudo?" Nicholas said.

"If you ever have a problem, just knock, twenty-four hours a day," Mr. Tupper said.

"We're here," Mrs. Tupper added.

"It's going to be a great year, boys."

"'Night now."

Nicholas shut the door behind them. "Where the hell did Spooner find them, the Goodwill?"

"They're sweet."

"Sweet? They're nightmares. I can't stand sincerity, it's so phony."

"I take it this is Mr. Tupper's first year?"

"And last, I hope, not that we'll be around. You see, Arthur, it would be an understatement to say that the Spooner School is strapped for cash. And so Mr. Spooner trolls around at these educational job fairs looking for people who will work for peanuts. Ergo Mr. Tupper. But mark my words—he won't make it to June. Listen, I often stay up very late, is that going to be a problem?" he asked, a little edge in his voice.

"With the light on?"

"Just this," he said, switching on a little clip-on lamp on his headboard.

"Nah."

He went back to *Naked Lunch*. I turned out the light and got into bed—the window was cracked and a soft breeze blew in; it smelled like the country, piney and fresh. I was so glad to be out of Collegiate, away from my parents, at a place where I was accepted, where I could meet a girl like Katrina. I knew it was only a new school, but in some way I felt like I'd dipped my toe into the water of the big world.

"Arthur?" Nicholas said in a whisper that sounded tinged with fear.

"Hmm?"

"Good night."

I WAS PULLED from sleep by a pebble pinging against my window. I looked out and saw Katrina gazing up at me.

"Come on out, Arthur!" she whispered, her pale, excited face lit by moonlight.

"What time is it?"

"Who cares? It's a beautiful night—and I have a bottle of Dom Pérignon." She held up the bottle.

"We might get caught."

"Who cares again."

"What if they hear me?"

"Oh don't be a goose, just jump."

It was about an eight-foot drop. What if I broke my leg? But I couldn't let Katrina know what a wimp I was, so I clambered out the window as quietly as I could, hung from the sill for a second, dropped, landed, and smashed my knee. Katrina, giggling, took my hand, pulled me up, and led me in a limping dash across the drive. We hoisted ourselves up onto the old stone wall and sat with our legs dangling, facing the lake.

"Isn't it exquisite, Arthur?"

It sure was—a still, cloudless night with a three-quarter moon, the lake flat, black, shimmering, while on the island the weeping willow kept its woeful watch.

"I know we're the Four Mouseketeers and all that, but let's you and I be very-very-*very* best friends this year," Katrina said. "You see, I don't believe you can be promiscuous with friendship. It's too precious. If you have lots of friends then it all becomes a big shallow wash. I prefer one deep friendship. What say, old chum?"

I was a little taken aback by this sudden offer, but I didn't want to hurt her feelings. Plus, and I hated myself for thinking this, she *was* Jean Clarke's daughter.

"Sure."

"Oh, thank you," she said, throwing her arms around my neck and kissing me on the cheek. I froze. "Will you relax."

"Katrina, I just got kicked out of one school."

"Oh, Noodles, nobody gets kicked out of this place. I mean, half the kids here were kicked out of someplace else."

"Were you?"

"Well, I was kicked out of L.A."

"By whom?"

"Daddy. He gave me the old heave-ho. Go East, bad girl. Get thee to a prep school."

"You mean because of the . . ."

"Yes, that boy trouble. You see, I went through a surfer-chick phase; the whole beach scene seemed so real compared to all the Bel Air la-de-da." She was quiet for a moment, sadness swept over her face, and when she spoke her voice was low. "And silly me, I thought it was love." Then she raked her fingers through her hair, shook her head, and was back to her sparkling self: "But whatever it was, it's ancient history—*finis!* Onward."

"I'm sorry."

"Sorry?"

"It sounds like you got hurt."

"This broad's tough, baby, she can handle it," she said in a gangster moll voice.

I wasn't sure how tough she was, but thought I should probably drop the subject. "So what does your dad do?" I asked, even though, as a rabid Jean Clarke fan, I knew the answer.

"Composes film scores; he's won two Oscars."

"Morris Felt?"

"The one and only, the human icicle famous for his lush, warm scores. Daddy-o has a major genius complex, acts like he's royalty, won't set foot in the kitchen, treats his help like slaves, it's awful. You should see his new wife, his fourth, Martina Von Aupperle. She's Austrian, wears her hair in a chignon—at breakfast! So skinny she can't walk over sidewalk grates, not that she'd be caught dead walking anywhere. She treats her darling stepdaughter like an unpleasant inconvenience. Runs the house like a machine. I think the old man has finally found his match." Katrina deftly pulled the gold foil off the champagne bottle and untwisted the wire mesh encircling the cork. "I've been opening Dom Pérignon since I was six." She eased out the cork and let it rip; foam bubbled out of the bottle and she brought it to her mouth and took a long swig. "I *adore* champagne," she said, handing me the bottle. I took a sip and grimaced as the bubbles flew up my nose. "You don't drink much, do you?"

I shook my head. "Do you want to go to college?"

"No, maybe, I don't know. But I am sick of everyone wanting to rush me into the business."

I knew from my obsessive reading of star biographies that "the business" was shorthand for show business. "Oh, are there people who want you to go into the business?" I asked, trying to sound casual but secretly thrilled to be using the term.

"Oh, Noodles, I've been singing at parties since I was in diapers. They say I have talent. I have an agent and all that. In fact, he called last week, there's some project in the works and they have their eye on me."

"What sort of project?"

"A Broadway musical, I gather, it's all very hush-hush at this stage."

"That's exciting."

"I suppose." For just a moment she looked frightened, then she took another swig.

"Well, maybe you should consider college then. Some of them are very liberal, you can make up your own curriculum." Show business sounded ten thousand times more appealing to me than college, but I wanted to be a good friend.

"You may be on to something there, old chum. I'll major in being scandalous. Anyway it's light years away, isn't it? So here's to a great year. You and me, Noodles." She took a swig and so did I.

Then she stood up on the wall and began to sing to me:

> Pack up all my care and woe
> Here I go, singing low
> Bye, bye blackbird

Her voice was lovely, more than lovely, with a distinctive throaty warmth and a touch of vibrato. And she had a presence that seemed to leap out of the night. She did a little soft-shoe on the stones, all grace and charm. I was captivated.

> Where somebody waits for me
> Sugar's sweet, so is he
> Bye, bye blackbird

Suddenly a light came on upstairs in the main house. Caught! We both dropped down on the far side of the wall, trying to contain our delicious champagne giggles.

2

THE NEXT MORNING the whole school gathered in the assembly hall, an immaculate white room flooded with morning light from a wall of windows that overlooked the lake. Mr. Spooner stood before us, waiting for us to settle so he could begin his welcoming words. He was so filled with clear bursting energy that he seemed electrified. The room grew silent, he opened his mouth to speak—and then Katrina blew in, a blur in black linen slacks, black cashmere sweater, black heels, black sunglasses, and earrings that looked like tiny Calder mobiles. She swept over to the seat I was saving, sat, pushed the sunglasses up on her head, and slapped on an "I'm paying attention" expression. A ripple ran through the room and a tiny smile played at the corners of Mr. Spooner's mouth.

"At the Spooner School we believe in creative education, an education based on unbridled expression. Let your spirit run freely over the geography of your soul. Each of you is a wellspring of intelligence, insight, and yes, glory, and together we are a magnificent water garden, nurturing one another's blooms." His eyes were crackling like sparklers, everyone was rapt, tapped into his spirit. "It's a fine, sturdy ship, you are the able-bodied crew, and today we set off on a glorious voyage. Rejoice and let us begin."

With that he lifted an old brass bell and clanged it, ringing in the school year.

There was a sharp beat where the room—the whole world it seemed—hung suspended.

Then everything was movement and we were off to our classes.

⁓

THE ART, MUSIC, and theater studios were in the main building, and all the other classes met in the guest cabins. This was where the senior class, all nine of us, headed for Discussion, a Spooner innovation where a student picked a topic and it was Discussed.

"You'll like Dr. Sophia Newcomb, she's pretty intense," Sapphire said as we walked across campus.

"She's Italian, from some aristocratic old family. That's her husband over there, he's descended from the founders of Connecticut or something," Nicholas said, pointing to a thin silver-haired gentleman in a blue blazer and ascot sitting on the front porch of the boys' dorm, smoking a cigarette in a holder, looking like he'd just stepped out of a scotch ad.

"He's very B-list Douglas Fairbanks," Katrina said.

"He drinks martinis for breakfast, always smells like raw onions, he eats them to disguise the booze, he fucks around a lot, he tried to ball me last year," Sapphire said. "His name's Cutter. I guess when you found Connecticut you name your kids Cutter and stuff."

Walking near us was Lenny Solberg, a swarthy day student who had a broad Slavic face with full lips, a cleft chin, and curly reddish-blond hair. Lenny was a bouncy, masculine kind of guy.

"Hey, hot stuff, how was your summer?" Sapphire asked him.

"It was pretty far out. I went to a wilderness camp out in British Columbia," Lenny said, and then he smiled—a ready, guileless smile that revealed a sexy snaggle tooth. When I saw that tooth my knees went a little weak.

Katrina leaned into my ear and whispered, "Arthur's been bitten by a little bug called love."

"That's ridiculous."

"It's written all over your mug, silly boy. And I don't blame you a whit, he's *trés* shagadelic."

We reached the cabin, filed in, and sat around a long table. Sophia Newcomb was sitting silently at the head of the table—a stout woman with rich black hair tucked into a tight bun and jabbed through with a tortoiseshell comb, olive skin, a full face crowned by a noble hooked nose, and huge dark eyes that were vats of wisdom and sadness. She watched us as we settled, filling the silence with great inchoate meaning.

"Well . . ." she began, in a voice that would make a sneeze sound profound. "For those of you who are new to the ways of Spooner, we will simply begin Discussion. Soon you will understand."

"Mick Jagger's lips," Sapphire tossed out.

The words hung in the air for a moment—Dr. Newcomb tilted her head in grave acknowledgment.

Silence.

Finally she repeated the words, sonorous and slow: "*Mick . . .
Jagger's . . . lips.*"

Another silence.

Then a Volvo girl blurted out, "I think Mick Jagger's lips are ugly,
they're gross, they're too . . . *big!*"

"Mick Jagger's lips are life," Nicholas said.

"Ah," Dr. Newcomb said significantly. You could tell that Nicholas
was her favorite.

"Oh, honestly, Nicholas, you always say things like that. Mick
Jagger's lips are *not* life, they're Mick Jagger's lips and he sings very
suggestive songs with them that are in bad taste," the Volvo said with
a little flick of her blond hair.

"Literal," Nicholas shot back.

Katrina burst in, "Mick's lips are loosey-goosey, they're trippy and fun
and giving a big 'fuck you' to the British class system. I mean, how dare
those Tory snobs look down at Mick, just because he wasn't born into
some moldy old family that's made marmalade for two hundred years?
It makes me damn mad, people should be judged for who they are. And
Mick is *fab*ulouso. Have you seen him perform? It's an orgasm."

She was so passionate and egalitarian, but more important, I
could tell from the way she said "Mick" that she'd met him.

Dr. Newcomb let out a weighty "Hmmmm."

"I want Mick Jagger's lips on my clit," Sapphire said throatily.

"That could be arranged," Katrina said.

Dr. Newcomb didn't bat an eye. "So, somehow these lips, these
extraordinary lips, have come to symbolize a generation, but *why?*"

"Because they're saying 'screw you' to the establishment?" I offered,
ever ready with an inane cliché.

"'Screw you' or 'I want to screw you'?" Nicholas asked.

A Volvo boy sat up straight, and said with frightening sincerity, "Obviously America is a morally corrupt society. I abhor the war in Vietnam, but we don't want to throw out the baby with the bathwater. There's no Nantucket in Russia, you know."

"Nantucket is hell on earth," Nicholas said.

"My car broke down there, we scored some incredible Jamaican," Lenny Solberg said.

"I prefer the Vineyard, it's integrated," the Volvo boy said smugly.

"What about Coney Island?" Lenny cracked.

"Coney Island is the saddest place in the world," I said, remembering one bleak winter Tuesday when I'd cut school and taken the A train out there.

"Did you find Coney Island sad or did Coney Island find *you* sad?" Dr. Newcomb asked, lighting a Pall Mall and taking a deep Jeanne Moreau–esque drag. This was apparently a signal—half the class pulled out cigarettes and lit up.

"Umm," I floundered.

"Coney Island found *you* sad, Arthur MacDougal, because you are sad, and that's why I love you," Katrina said.

I felt myself blush.

"Despair," Nicholas said.

"Yes?" Dr. Newcomb encouraged.

"Hiroshima, Vietnam, Coney Island, Ezra Pound, the knife in the water," Nicholas said.

Dr. Newcomb, excited, took a deep pull on her Pall Mall, leaned forward on the table, and as she exhaled looked at each of us in turn, to make sure we had heard, had understood.

KATRINA CALLED FOR a cab after classes and she and I rode into Westridge. It was small, prosperous, self-satisfied, filled with flowerboxes and flags, very Early American, with spinning wheels and rocking cradles out in front of the antique shops.

"It looks like a yard sale at Betsy Ross's place," Katrina said. She looked wildly glamorous and out of place—I mean, heads turned— in her black outfit and a red leather jacket.

The hardware store, even though it had potpourri in its window, looked and smelled wonderfully authentic, with a worn wood floor and aisles jammed with pipes, nails, tools, and other stuff that I would never buy or use. The chubby young man who mixed up our gallons of Abba-Dabba was completely awed by Katrina, and she charmed him with naïve questions and gushing gratitude.

After dinner the four of us donned smocks, pushed all the tables and chairs to the middle of the room, put down drop cloths, and set to work painting the dining room. I had never painted anything before and my enthusiasm lasted all of twenty minutes. I mean, it was *work*. Couldn't we have just hired someone? But Katrina found a portable record player, put on the Beatles, and pretty soon I found that I was actually enjoying myself. And the room was transforming, the dark wood giving way to warmth and color. We had just gotten on the first coat when Mr. Spooner appeared from upstairs.

"What have we here?" he asked.

"Well, when we're done we'll have an Abba-Dabba dining room," Katrina said from her perch on a ladder.

Mr. Spooner smiled that enigmatic smile of his. "How glorious! And how was the first day of classes?"

"Wonderful."

"Great."

"Scrumptious."

"Ah, the feast has begun. Well, I won't interrupt you." He turned to leave and then turned back, looked at the four of us, and said, "I walk with love along the way / And oh it is a holy day."

After he was gone we fell into a silence as we painted. It was a group silence, and it was filled with something I was pretty sure was love.

3

MY LAST CLASS that first week was Mr. Tupper's Our World.

"Well now, everyone, you're all going to have to help me out here a little bit, after all I'm just a hick from Minnesota," Mr. Tupper began in his 'please love me, I'm a friendly old codger' way. His beard sported a piece of spinach left over from lunch—it moved when he talked. "I'm a bit more of a traditionalist when it comes to education, but I'm willing to give Edward Spooner's theories a go. So Our World is going to be freeform, as they say, your class as much as mine. I want us to explore the issues that affect man as a community animal, the family of man, if you will."

He waited for a response. There was none.

As Katrina and I had walked to the cabin we'd noticed a posse of kids emerging from the woods, and now fully half the class looked stoned to me, sitting there with glassy red eyes and half-opened mouths.

"Let me tell a little story that illustrates some of the issues I'm talking about. Just last spring my wife and I were on our way to a political dinner, we're active in the Democratic Farm Labor party in our hometown. We were running a little late, I was going, oh, maybe five miles over the speed limit when we were pulled over by a sheriff's deputy, said we were speeding. Five miles an hour. I tried to reason with the fellow, but he was being very hard line, told me to get in the back of the police car. I opened the cruiser's back door and there was a hat on the seat with a little sign that read 'contributions.' I looked at that hat and that sign, I mean, this was *wrong*, this was corruption, bribery, exactly the kind of thing I'd spent my whole life fighting."

He paused and looked at us all, making sure we knew how repugnant he found it.

"I wanted to grab that hat and crumple it up, tell the man to take me in, I was going to blow this thing sky high. But I hesitated—that money could have been for a new baby or someone's medical bills, these things happen ... I threw a five-dollar bill in the hat. You see, we were late for the dinner, my wife was cold, it was a chilly night."

Mr. Tupper, spinach-flecked beard and watery eyes, frayed jacket and dingy white shirt, looked at us with a sheepish smile. I realized he was asking us to forgive him.

Just then Katrina piped up, "Oh, Mr. Tupper, you did *absolutely* the right thing. We have to pick our battles, *n'est pas*? And this one was certainly *not* worth the trouble. Those troopers were grubby little men and you're *better* than that. Save your fire for a worthy opponent."

He smiled at her with such gratitude that I thought he might cry.

"And Mr. Tupper?" Katrina said shyly.

"Yes, Katrina."

"This has nothing to do with Our World, but you have a little bit of lunch left on your beard," she said in the gentlest voice, as if having food dangling off your face was a charming and sympathetic predicament, one that befell only the most brilliant of men. Then she took out a handkerchief, walked around the table, and tenderly brushed off the bit of spinach. Mr. Tupper melted under her ministrations.

"Thank you, young lady." He turned to the class, his confidence renewed, and said: "Lyndon Baines Johnson." He let the name hang there for a moment. "Quite a figure. Met him once in St. Paul, in the men's room at the union hall. I was relieving myself, in he came with two Secret Service men. He said 'Howdy' and went into a stall. Wasn't at all shy about . . . you know." He leaned forward, elbows on the table—the raconteur. "Well, there I was at the urinal and the president of the United States starts talking to me from the stall. 'Can't stand that George Hamilton fella. Too damn tan, looks like a fairy, but Lynda Bird's got a bug up her ass and what the hell can I do, I'm only her father. Goddamnit, there's no toilet paper!' There was a shelf up over my head with rolls of paper on it, I reached up and grabbed one, turned and stuck it under the side of the stall. 'Here you go, Mr. President,' I said. 'Why, thank you, son. Now listen, you ever need any help with anything, anything at all, you give me a call, y'hear?' In return for handing him a roll of toilet paper, I earned a political chit from the president of the Unites States."

He leaned back and smiled, sure he had impressed us.

"LBJ is a war criminal," someone said.

"Well now, I'm no fan of the Vietnam War, but he is our President," Mr. Tupper said, taken aback.

But it was too late; the dogs of stoned spoiled teenagers had been unleashed:

"Johnson is a pig."

"U.S. out of Vietnam."

"Freedom now."

"Marijuana is more important than Congress, at least it gets you high."

"Lady Bird takes acid."

"Lady Bird *is* acid."

Mr. Tupper sat there, stunned, and then I saw his eyes narrow as his shock edged toward anger.

4

IT WAS A Monday night, about three weeks into the school year. I was lying on my bed reading a biography of Jean Harlow, one of my favorite movie stars. The book was upsetting because it blamed her death at the tragically young age of twenty-six, from a probably treatable infection, on her Christian Scientist mother, who wouldn't allow any doctors to see her. I wondered if I should bring this up with Mr. Spooner.

The pay phone down at the end of the hall rang. And rang again. If you were the only one around, it was considered bad form not to answer it and take a message—after all, it might be someone's dealer. So I reluctantly went and got it.

"Hello."

"Arthur?"

"Hi, Mom," I said, slipping into my protective shell.

"How are you, darling?"

"Fine."

"How's Spooner?"

"It's good. I like it."

"Oh, that's wonderful. Have you made some friends?"

"Yes, I have as a matter of fact," I said. I knew my lack of friends at Collegiate had Mom and Dad a little worried, frantic actually.

"Oh, darling, I'm so happy to hear that. It's Arthur, Charles. He's made some friends. Oh, I just had a feeling about that place, that it was right for you. So many nice children go there." *Nice* was Mom's code word for "socially connected."

Just then Mr. Tupper came in the front door. He sniffed at the air in an exaggerated way, scrutinized my eyes, and then continued on his way.

"How are you and Dad?" I asked, wanting to change the subject. I was never comfortable talking about me with my parents.

"Wonderful. Your father's project is full steam ahead." I'd heard that one before. Dad was always getting fired up about things like Indian mounds in the Midwest or legends of Eskimo storytelling—he'd travel, do research, plan books and documentaries. Then his interest would fade and we'd all go to Europe on vacation. His latest obsession was Storyville, the New Orleans neighborhood where prostitution was legal for a few decades around the turn of the twentieth century. "He's obsessed. I never see the man. Who can blame him? Storyville is so fascinating. Legalized prostitution is a marvelous idea. Did you know they had little blue books that listed all the women and their specialties? And the music, all that jazzy jazz. Where would America be without its Negroes?"

"Blacks," I corrected.

"Blacks," Mom said. "Listen, darling, we want to drive up next Friday and take you out to dinner. Betty Stein discovered a Japanese place in Bethel, she says it's delicious fun, it's an eighteenth-century temple imported screen by screen. One sits on the floor, so do wear clean socks. How does that sound?"

"Fine," I said, taking the path of least resistance. Then I had an idea to make the outing more bearable. "Can I bring someone along?"

"Is it a girl perhaps?"

I tensed up. "No, Mom, it isn't. Well, it is a girl, but not a girl-*friend*."

I heard her pull on her cigarette. "I just meant, you know, a school-mate, a chum, someone you'd like us to meet."

"Okay."

"We'll be up around seven. Oh, darling?"

"Yes, Mom?"

"This is a nice place. Please do wear a tie."

"Mom, we're napalming innocent babies in Vietnam and you're telling me to *wear a tie*?"

"I'm so proud of you, Arthur."

"Thanks, Mom. Listen, I've been looking at photography books, I'd love a camera."

"Would you? Of course, darling. See you at seven."

THE OLD FRONT parlor of the main house served as the school library. It was book-lined, with a worn Oriental carpet, a fireplace, several reading chairs, a bench, and a large oak table. This was Katrina's favorite place; she pronounced it "cozy and creepy at the same time," and sure enough there she was, sitting at the table, absorbed in *Jane Eyre*. She looked up at me and smiled. "This book is amazing."

I sat in one of the chairs, not wanting to interrupt her, and thumbed through a copy of *Life,* marveling at pictures of Liza-with-a-*z* cavorting in her new Manhattan apartment, which seemed to be furnished entirely in plastic.

Katrina looked at me over the top of the book. "I'm *obsessed* with the Brontës, Arthur. Sophia Newcomb turned me on to them. They were *so* amazing, there were four children: Anne, Emily, Charlotte, and Branwell, and they grew up in this isolated country parsonage way up in the middle of the moors and had nothing to amuse them but their imaginations. They invented an imaginary African kingdom! And they wrote about it in *tiny* books in *tiny* handwriting. They even invented their own *language*. Maybe we should do that, Noodles. Poor Branwell became a morphine addict. They all died young."

Katrina's passion was contagious—I imagined the Brontë siblings, borderline mad on the moors, running around in a fever of invention. Branwell sounded the most romantic—the words "morphine addict" conjured delicious images of indolence, of long dreamy days that drifted toward the soft evening.

Katrina read aloud, "'It was now the sweetest hour of the twenty-four: Day its fervid fires had wasted, and dew fell cool on panting plain and scorched summit.'" The words hung in the air for a moment. Then she closed the book and stood up. "Come on," she said, grabbing my hand.

Katrina led me down to the lake, the night was mild, moonless, the sky wide open and tossed with stars. She turned to me with a face that looked half-mad with happiness, "Oh, Arthur, isn't it divine?" She took out her flask, took a deep pull, and then held it out to me; I shook my head. She shrugged and took another long

swallow. Then she slipped out of her clothes her skin was very
white, her hips flared a little, she had small breasts. She looked so
vulnerable against the night, I had a sudden unsettling urge to go
to her, caress her, possess her, all of her. She slipped into the water
and disappeared. When she came up she was a little ways out from
shore—she tossed her head and grinned. "Come on in!"

"Aren't you freezing?"

"Feels heavenly. Come on."

I looked around nervously. Katrina was paddling on her back,
looking up at the stars. "Come on, Artie," she said, her voice echoing off the water. *Artie?*

"Do you think there are snapping turtles?"

"Artie-is-a-chicken."

It wasn't the first time I'd been called a chicken. Usually I just
walked away, but for some reason this time I wanted to prove her
wrong. I bit down, stripped, and dove in—the water was scrotum-
shrinking cold. I never did this kind of thing, it was very un-me. I
swam over to Katrina.

"Isn't it exquisite?" she said.

She sure was, her skin and eyes glistening. As for the water, well,
I doubted I could talk through chattering teeth, so I just tried to
smile.

"Swim, it'll warm you up." She splashed me and laughed. "Do
you like that name—Artie?"

"No one's ever called me that before."

"It's *our* name then. It suits you." Then she splashed me again and
started to sidestroke toward the island. I followed, and sure enough
I did start to warm up. Exhilarated, I looked up at the stars and then
at their reflection in the black water. I caught up with Katrina.

"Have you always been so . . . ?"

"So what?"

"So brave."

She laughed. "I'm not brave, silly, I just like to have fun."

She reached the island and got out. I followed. My body instantly one big goose bump, I jumped up and down. Katrina was climbing the weeping willow, was barely visible through the hanging branches.

"You want to come out to dinner with my folks on Friday?" I called.

"Sure."

"What are you doing?"

"I'm climbing this tree. What are your parents like?"

"They're nice. They mean well, I guess. What about yours?"

"They're famous and self-obsessed. I'm not real to them," she said, gathering in a bunch of branches.

"Why not?"

"Because I'm growing up. They can't handle that. Mom liked me when I was little and could be dressed up like a doll and paraded around. Now I'm just a wrinkle meter to her. Dad never said ten words to me; he just holed up in his studio and lived out his Mozart fantasy. The only time they pay attention to me is when I fuck up, which is probably *why* I fuck up."

"You mean like with the boyfriend they didn't approve of?"

"Arthur, I told you that topic is off-limits," she said with surprising vehemence.

"I'm sorry."

"Never be sorry!" she said. And then she leaped from her perch, swinging out over the water from the rope of willow branches—she let go, flew through the air, splashed down, and came up laughing.

"You have *got* to try that!"

"No way," I said. In fact, I was wishing the island had a little gazebo with a heated towel rack, not to mention a footbridge back to shore.

"You can't sleep out there, Artie."

She had a point. I looked down at my dick—hardly Errol Flynn–esque in the best of times, it had retracted to a tiny peanut. I didn't blame it. Katrina splashed me, the drops felt like stinging nettles. I steeled myself, dove in, and swam underwater to her. I grabbed her leg, she kicked, I held on, tickling her foot, I dove down and tickled her armpits, we rolled around underwater, jabbing and squirming.

We came up for air, laughing, splashing, spurting—and with a jolt stronger than the cold of the water I realized that I'd never been this happy before.

5

DINNER WAS SUPPOSED to be for boarding students only, but like most rules at Spooner this one was basically ignored. One night about a week after my swim with Katrina, Lenny Solberg and a sophomore named Jeanie were hanging out. Jeanie was cute, on the pudgy side, had a round face with dimples, pale smooth skin. She and Lenny were sort of an item. I was carrying a ridiculous schoolboy crush for Lenny, a delusion stoked by Katrina, who assured me that Lenny "liked" me. When I asked her how she could tell, she said, "The nose knows."

I listened as they gossiped about Spooner alumni—Marcus Lipps was running around with the Andy Warhol crowd in the city, he was very beautiful and never slept; Michael Berg was a "genius" who made 8-millimeter films and was in Quintana Roo doing mescaline and reenacting Mayan rituals; Rodina Paulson had done a poetry reading with Allen Ginsburg and slashed her wrists in Harvard Square. They all sounded so fearless and creative. I didn't mention that my big ambition was to manage a movie theater that only showed the classics and served real popcorn.

After dinner we all went back into the woods. It was a beautiful mild night, the waning moon hanging low in the sky, casting spindly shadows across the Spot. The air had a gentle nip, fragrant with dirt and leaves and bark, and the woods around us seemed endless and a deep-layered black; scurrying and cawing and rustling punctuated the calm. I felt safe, even cozy, with my new friends.

Sapphire gathered some twigs and sticks and made a fire in the rock hearth, we sat in a circle, the flames' glow danced on our faces, a joint was passed. By this time I was pretty good at pretending to take a toke.

"This was probably an Indian campsite two hundred years ago," Sapphire said.

Katrina smiled. "I think the Indians could probably have done a little better."

Nicholas leaned into the fire. "Indians didn't know about lying until we came."

Sapphire's eyes welled with tears. "We destroyed their culture."

"With God on our side," Nicholas said.

"Manifest destiny," Lenny said.

Nicholas exhaled a stream of pot smoke and said, "Manifest *greed*."

"It's all going to change, man," Lenny said.

"It is going to change, *we're* going to change it," Sapphire said, anger behind her tears.

"We're going to knock those rich old white men right out of their ivory jet bomber," Nicholas said fiercely.

They reminded me of an anti-war rap session I'd seen in a TV documentary.

"Drugs, love, rock 'n' roll," Sapphire said.

Katrina sat up. "Now you've got me interested."

"I ain't going to study war no more," Jeanie said, putting a hand on Lenny's thigh.

"Are you experienced, have you ever been experienced before?" Lenny said. He kissed Jeanie; she opened her mouth to him.

"The bomb," Nicholas said.

"Why?" Sapphire asked, looking six years old.

Nicholas looked into the flames. "Money, power, weird shit."

Lenny and Jeanie were making out on the ground.

"People disintegrated in Hiroshima, in an instant, they just dematerialized," Sapphire said.

"Those were the lucky ones," Nicholas said.

Jeanie had her blouse off; she had large, sloping breasts. Lenny put his mouth on one of her nipples. I couldn't believe no one was saying anything. She was opening his pants and reaching inside.

"Someday someone's going to drop another one; that's the way man is," Sapphire said.

Nicholas nodded. "They have whole departments in the Pentagon doing nothing but figuring out where and when."

"And how to survive. What a joke," Sapphire said.

Katrina said, "I remember Jane Russell telling us they'd watch the tests out in the Nevada desert after a day of filming, drink their cocktails and watch the A-bombs explode. How posh. Now they're all coming down with cancer."

Jeanie and Lenny were naked; I mean, they had no clothes on *at all*. Right in front of us! I'd never seen real live naked people before—it was the sexiest thing I'd ever seen (of course, it didn't have much competition—I masturbated to the bodybuilding ads in the back of my comic books). Lenny was on his knees between Jeanie's legs and he was excited in a *big* way. Wow! The flames threw flickering orange highlights over their bodies.

"How could they do it, how could they actually sit in a laboratory and make that bomb? Assholes!" Sapphire spit out.

"The military industrial complex," Nicholas said.

"We have to fight them, don't we?" Katrina said.

"We will, and we'll win," Sapphire said. "Love is more powerful than hate."

A few feet away, Lenny and Jeanie were proving her point. He slid into her. I didn't know who I was more embarrassed for, me or them. They certainly didn't seem embarrassed for themselves, so I don't know what I was worrying about.

"I want to spend next summer working against the war," Sapphire said.

"Me, too," Katrina said. "In Malibu."

I didn't want to look at Lenny and Jeanie, but my eyes sure did. Jeanie threw her head back on the ground and moaned. Lenny seemed so nonchalant, looking down cooly at their union, the tip of his tongue came out and rested lightly on his upper lip—oh God, was that sexy. Jeanie started to move her body, to match his thrusts. I managed to drag my gaze back to the fire.

"Drugs are weapons of peace," Sapphire said.

Katrina smiled, "Especially Dom Pérignon."

"The doors of perception," Nicholas added.

"The Doors," I threw in, glad I could contribute (although my musical tastes ran more to Cole Porter).

"*Come on, baby, light my fire . . .*" Nicholas sang, dipping a branch into the flames.

"... *Try to set the night on fire*," Sapphire sang.

Nicholas lifted the branch from the fire, a tiny flame burning at its tip, in stark relief against the night. He stood up and started to circle the Spot, waving the burning branch in front of him, throwing tiny waves of orange light.

"Oh fun, a conga line!" Katrina said, jumping up and getting in line behind him. Sapphire and I followed. Katrina turned, nodded toward Lenny and Jeanie, and made a "Can-you-*believe*-those-two?" face.

"*Come on, baby, light my fire / Try to set the night on fire*," Nicholas sang.

I was glad I was last in line; it made it easier to keep an eye on things. Lenny was now on the ground, Jeanie on top of him, her feet beside his hips, riding him, and he was leaning up, staring at her face, his cool cast off. She looked over at us—at me! I didn't know if I should smile encouragement, pant like a dog, or pretend I wasn't watching.

"*Come on, baby, light my fire / Try to set the night on fire*," we all sang, letting the flaming stick pull the words out of us. So *this* is free love, I thought. Well, at least now I knew what all the hoopla was about.

Lenny was thrusting up now—Jeanie's high-pitched screams began, grew louder and louder, burying his low moans, it sounded like she was dying or giving birth to triplets. I guess this was part of the Spooner education Edward spoke of. I mean, nothing like this ever happened at Collegiate.

"*Come on, baby, light my fire / Try to set the night on fire.*"

Jeanie's screams roller-coastered into a lower register and finally tapered off to barely audible little groans. Then she collapsed onto Lenny and they curled together, purring like kittens.

The four of us stopped marching and looked at each other, suddenly sheepish.

"Where's Margaret Mead when you need her?" Nicholas asked.

6

"It's charming," Mom said, looking around my room.

"Here," Dad said, handing me an expensive-looking camera. I took it out of the case and examined it—it looked complicated.

"Thanks," I said, putting it on my dresser top.

"Here's the booklet," he said.

The booklet was thick and full of technical terms and drawings. I was so bad at all that, I should have just gone out and bought an Instamatic.

"So, who are we taking?" Mom asked. She perched on one of the little wooden chairs, crossed her legs, and lit a True Blue. Dad stood by the door puffing his dark Nat Sherman and looking distracted.

"Katrina Felt."

"And what does her father do?" Mom said. That was always her first question—you could set your watch by it.

"He's a movie composer, Morris Felt," I said nonchalantly, knowing Katrina's pedigree would send them both into heat.

"Oh wait, is her mother Jean Clarke?" Mom asked, perking up as expected.

"Yes, Mom, her mother is Jean Clarke."

Mom and Dad exchanged a glance, and I watched as their interest in our dinner outing soared.

"Jean Clarke is great friends with the Coopers," Mom said.

"You don't say," I said. I didn't want Mom to be all over Katrina, fawning and dropping names and trying to take her away from me.

"She's a pretty good actress, actually," Dad said.

"She can act," Mom said.

The way Mom and Dad delivered their opinions, you'd think they'd invented the wheel, discovered the New World, and directed *Citizen Kane*.

"Sis Cooper says she's impossible when she drinks. Repeats herself—endlessly, ad infinitum, ad nauseam," Mom said.

"You guys," I whined. I could feel frustration boiling up in me. I wished I hadn't asked Katrina along—I didn't want to expose her to my folks.

Mom laughed. "Don't worry, darling."

"I smell parents," Nicholas said, walking into the room, taking a baggie of pot from the desk and holding it up for my folks to see. "Don't stop your psychological maneuvering on my account, I'm just on my way out. I'd offer you a joint but I can tell you're from the martini generation. Your son is sweet, but a mess. I foresee an institution in his future, and I don't mean an ivy-covered one." I suppressed a smile, secretly delighted that my folks were seeing what cool and clever new friends I had. "I'm off to get blitzed with some of the gang, it's nightly entertainment here at Spooner. It's been such a pleasure."

The room felt empty after he left.

"What a thoroughly ill-mannered child," Mom said.

"His father is Alfred Meyers of Meyers Press," I said casually.

"Oh," Mom said flatly, trying to disguise her surprise and interest.

"Not a bad house," Dad said.

"Of course we know Alfred Meyers. We were at the Grand in Rome at the same time. Had drinks. Basically a vulgar man. Flaunts his education." Mom paused before delivering the killer: "I believe his father sold pickles."

I lay down on my bed and looked up at the ceiling, dreading how they'd behave in front of Katrina.

Dad walked over, looked down at me, and smiled, a kind smile. He seemed to know what I was thinking. "What are you going to photograph?"

"I don't know. Just around, I guess," I said, sulking.

"That's wonderful," Mom said. I waited for her to drop the name of some famous photographer they knew, but she didn't, she smiled warmly.

I never could figure those two out.

Katrina appeared in the doorway—she had on ruby-red lipstick and black eyeliner, and was wearing a short black skirt, a crisp white oxford shirt, a black cashmere cardigan on her shoulders, and black flats. With her enormous eyes, white skin, and black hair, the effect was stunning, grown-up, sophisticated, as if she'd stepped off the pages of *Harper's Bazaar*.

Mom and Dad just stared for a second.

"Hi," Katrina said with a shy, disarming smile.

"You must be Katrina," Mom said, rising to take her hand. "Esme MacDougal."

"Charles MacDougal. What a pleasure."

"It's so nice to meet both of you," Katrina said with dazzling charm, before turning to me with a wry, "Hi, Arthur."

"Hi, Katrina."

Mom got her bearings. "Shall we go?"

⁓

THE JAPANESE TEMPLE/RESTAURANT was set on a small hill and surrounded by an expanse of raked pebbles with larger rocks stuck here and there in an artful way that made me think profound thoughts, like how hard it must be to keep it looking that perfect.

"Isn't this fun?" Mom said as we slipped out of our shoes and were led to our own little screened cubicle, where we sat on the floor around a low table. Mom's toenails were painted red and made her look rich. Our waitress, festive in kimono and wig, bowed and left, but not before Dad had ordered saki for all.

Katrina snuggled happily into her cushion and I imagined we were brother and sister. She was a lot more fun than my real sister, Ann, a humorless intellectual who was a sophomore at Antioch.

"So, we and your mother share mutual friends," Mom said as she started to hit the saki.

"What a small world," Katrina said, and smiled. I realized how much she wanted them to like her.

"The Coopers, Mark and Sis. I believe he produced one of her movies," Mom said.

"I don't know them. I'm sure they're very nice people," Katrina said, taking a sip of sake. "Arthur and I like Spooner, don't we?"

I nodded. The whole parent thing felt different with Katrina along: I felt less vulnerable, confused, frustrated, less like a loser.

"What's your mother working on now?"

Katrina's expression changed, for a moment she looked very young and terribly lonely. "I don't know. I haven't talked to her in . . . a little while. She sent me an Hermès pocketbook, so I think she's in Paris." She ran her fingers through her hair and gave her head a little shake. "Maybe I should call her secretary and find out. 'Hello, Matt, it's Katrina, just where *the hell* is my mother?'" Then she laughed, all insouciance, but her huge dark eyes were still sad.

Mom and Dad lit cigarettes.

"Katrina's reading *Jane Eyre*," I said.

"Ah, I remember staying up all night reading that book," Mom said.

"What are your plans for next year, Katrina?" Dad asked.

Katrina looked down and smoothed out her woven-grass placemat. "I really don't know, there's some talk of a musical, Broadway."

"Have you heard any more about that?" I asked.

"Actually, my agent called again, it's a Kander and Ebb show, and there's a part they think I might be right for."

"Katrina, that's fantastic," I said.

"Do you know Kander and Ebb?" Mom asked.

"Well, sure, from parties, you know." Once again she ran her fingers through her hair and shook her head. "But Arthur has been encouraging me to think about college." She sounded sincere and a bit at sea, as if she wanted my parents to guide her.

"I know Arthur is going to apply to colleges out west," Dad said.

"He wants to get as far away from his dear old family as he can. Don't you, Arthur?" Mom said in a slightly taunting tone.

"I'd like to see some of the country."

"The people are very narrow-minded out west. It's dusty and they carry guns," Mom said

"I was thinking more like San Francisco, Mom. Real dusty."

"There are no decent schools in San Francisco," Mom said.

"With my grades that's not a problem." I was basically a straight-C student.

Mom ignored my comment. When it came to me or Ann, Mom basically ignored anything on the down side.

"San Francisco is a wonderful town," Katrina said.

"Oh, does your mother spend time there?" Mom asked.

"No. I ran away when I was fourteen and spent a week living in Golden Gate Park."

"How adventuresome," Mom managed.

"One night I was on top of Telegraph Hill," Katrina began, her voice growing soft and dreamy. "It was a full moon and the fog was rolling in through the Golden Gate—this huge finger of fog creeping in, spreading out over the bay, undulating over Alcatraz, covering the world with a glowing silver cloud. Oh, San Francisco—it's full of magic, and nameless lurking sorrow. I know my Artie would love it there."

I was elated that Katrina had claimed me; my folks looked a bit dazed.

There was a long pause.

Mercifully a chef arrived, wearing a huge chef hat. He bowed, lit something under the table's built-in wok, and started to chop vegetables in fast motion.

"The Japanese are so Asian," Mom said.

The blur of the chef's motions obliterated the need to talk. He threw some oil into the wok and started to toss in vegetables, which sizzled and bounced.

"I have to use the ladies room. Excuse me," Katrina said. She stood up, straightened her skirt, and left.

"Interesting girl," Mom said, champing at the bit.

"She's pretty adorable," Dad said, to Mom's annoyance.

"Must be *terribly difficult* having Jean Clarke and Morris Felt for parents."

That was so like Mom, to trash two talented, successful people—she had this weird need to feel superior to everyone. And did she think it was *terribly easy* to have her and Dad for parents?

"I think Katrina's wonderful. And you should hear her sing," I said.

"Are you and she . . . ?" Mom asked, trying to sound casual.

"No, Mom, we're not, we're friends."

"How modern." Mom picked up her chopsticks—she'd had quite enough of Katrina Felt for the moment. Then she put them down and turned to me. "Arthur, your father and I are worried about you," she said, a note of triumph in her voice.

Uh-oh, here it comes: the you-never-have-a-girlfriend talk. My belly turned to jello. My folks tried not to show it, but I knew that I was a big disappointment to them—for all their artsy, liberal pronouncements, what they really wanted was a lawyer, an architect, someone scrubbed and Brooks Brothersy with a bright wife and a place out in Amagansett. What they got was me: isolated, odd, anxious. I couldn't bear the thought of further deepening their disappointment by adding *homosexual* to the mix. Or was I just making excuses for my own cowardice? I looked at the food snap-crackle-popping in the wok.

"Aren't we, Charles?" Mom said.

Dad nodded dutifully. I just kept eyeballing that food dance. The chef tossed in cubes of beef that quickly singed and browned.

"You seem to lack . . . direction," Mom said with breathtaking originality.

I was so relieved that s-e-x wasn't the subject that I smiled.

"We're serious about this, Arthur," Mom said.

They were both looking at me with identical we-love-you-but-please-shape-up-you're-freaking-us-out expressions. It felt like there was a thick glass wall between us.

"I'm sorry," was all I could manage.

"Your father has something to say to you," Mom said.

This was something I'd never heard before, the real reason for the lack-of-direction song and dance. The seriousness level at the table skyrocketed. Dad looked miserable. The chef silently scooped the woked food onto plates and put them in front of us. He bowed and left, sliding the screen door closed behind him. I was alone in the little bamboo room with my folks and they were about to tell me something that I sensed was important. I changed position and the matting scrunched under me, I could hear the muffled chatter of other diners, the air smelled of bamboo, tea, and sesame oil. Dad took a bite of his food.

"Charles!" Mom snapped.

Like a guilty kid, Dad put down his chopsticks. He hated serious discussions even more than I did. The door slid open and Katrina sat back down. Mom frowned a not-so-tiny frown.

"Hi," Katrina said. I could smell gin on her breath.

"We thought we'd lost you," Mom said.

"I took a little walk. There's a beautiful garden out back. A pond with huge goldfish. Umm, this looks yummy."

"They may have been carp," Mom said.

We all started to eat. The food was delicious, the vegetables crisp and bursting, the beef moist and melting. "This is nirvana," Katrina said, unashamedly using her fork instead of the chopsticks, giving me courage to abandon my sixes-and-sevens struggle and do the same.

"Umm," Dad agreed happily, the hot seat unplugged.

"This is a lovely place, but have you seen some of our fellow diners? It looks like a convention of insurance brokers," Katrina said. Holding up her forefingers, she outlined a square.

Mom tried not to smile at Katrina's take on the clientele, but I knew she liked it—after all, it implied that our little foursome was superior.

"Well, Katrina, this *is* Fairfield County."

"I thought Fairfield County was full of artists and eccentric old rich ladies."

"Well, for every artist there are a hundred stodgy Republicans," Mom said. "Is this your first time living in the East?"

Katrina nodded. "Yes, I love it, I feel very at home here. Thanks to your wonderful son." She put her arm through mine and rested her head on my shoulder. I felt so proud to have it there. I wondered vaguely what Dad wanted to talk about, but with Katrina by my side I had at least momentary confidence that I could handle it, whatever it was.

Mom looked at Katrina with a slightly startled expression on her face, then she looked at me. Did I see anger in her eyes? Or was it sadness? Then she looked away, almost as if she was dismissing us both, and said to Dad, "Betty Stein was absolutely right, the food here is superb."

Under the table, Katrina squeezed my knee.

7

ONE NIGHT IN late October, I was fast asleep when I felt a hand stroking my hair.

"Artie, darling, I'm sorry to wake you, but I couldn't sleep, I've got a terrible case of the nasties," Katrina whispered. She lay down and snuggled up next to me.

"What time is it?"

"I dunno. Late. Scary time. The demons are out." She took my arm and wrapped it around her middle, snuggling closer.

A match struck across the room, a flash in the dark, and Nicholas lit a cigarette.

"Welcome to the funhouse," he whispered.

"I'm sorry, Nicholas, did I wake you?" Katrina whispered.

"Hardly. For some of us, the demons are out every night." He got up and lit a candle on the dresser top. He got back in bed and the three of us lay there in the flickering candlelight.

"Let's tell each other secrets," Katrina whispered.

There was a pause. Then Nicholas asked, "Do you want to hear about my mother?"

I knew his mother had killed herself, but that was all I knew. "Okay," I said.

Nicholas sat up in bed and began: "Mary, our maid, discovered Mom. She was late for a party at the Guggenheim, Dad was there, waiting. He called. I was up in my room, jerking off with this Swedish porno magazine my friend Jake from Riverdale Country Day had given me. I was looking at this picture of this skinny blond, very Scandinavian, very May Britt, a little too bony. She was masturbating herself with a pickle. The lighting was terrible, harsh, there was all this cheap-looking Scandinavian furniture in the room, she was on the floor and this naked, out-of-shape guy was sitting on the edge of the bed watching her. He wasn't even hard. The picture was not a turn-on, although it was fascinating culturally. I was just about to turn the page. In fact, I had the page between my fingers—that was when I heard Mary scream."

Nicholas's voice had that late-night tone, vivid and private. He paused, the candlelight waved across the ceiling.

"Mary's been with us since before I was born—she practically brought me up. She's from Gadsden, Alabama via Chicago. She doesn't do much anymore, but Dad keeps her on. He's been pretty good to her, actually. I'd never heard her scream before. She's a pretty tough lady. My first thought was that the house was on fire, then *burglar* flashed through my mind. I tossed the magazine and pulled up my pants. My room is on the third floor, Mom and Dad had the whole second. Mary was on the landing, clasping her hands, moving her head back and forth, like she was trying to figure out what to do. She looked up at me and said, 'Don't go in there. Nicholas.' That was when I knew. 'She's my mother,' I said.

"She was in the bathroom, hanging from the shower rod. She was all dressed up, this long blue dress, very tasteful, makeup, she even had on her perfume—Chanel No. 5. That was what hit me first, the perfume; she'd put on a little too much."

He laughed, a short bitter laugh. Katrina took my hand in both of hers and held it to her chest.

"I knew she was unhappy. She used to paint, we used to spend summers on the Cape, Truro, she loved it there, she'd wear shorts and T-shirts all summer, stick me in this basket on the front of her bike and we'd ride into town for fresh corn. She was very pretty, she was always smiling back then. Then Dad got really rich, we started going to the Hamptons, he started having affairs, maybe it was just getting old that got to her. Who fucking knows, man? But there she was, a little late for the Guggenheim."

The story was so sad, and so shocking, but I also found its drama thrilling—and I was proud that he had chosen to tell us.

"I'm sorry, Nicholas," I said.

"Me too," Katrina said in a tiny kind voice.

"You ever see anybody hung?'

"No."

"Well, the neck leans over, her chin was deep in her collarbone. She was dead, that can I tell you. Her eyes were closed. She didn't look peaceful—she just looked dead. After a while I said, 'Hey, Mom.' She didn't answer me."

That laugh again.

In the silence that followed the laugh we could hear him cry.

And then stop abruptly.

"Fuck, man, it's all an existential nightmare." He got up and walked into the bathroom, tossing his cigarette in the toilet, a sharp little hiss marking its watery end.

Just then the door to our room flew open, the light was switched on, and Mr. Tupper was standing there. He was tousled and bleary-eyed, wearing a bathrobe.

"What the hell is going on in here?" he barked.

Katrina and I yanked ourselves up to sitting positions.

"Nothing, Mr. Tupper, we were just talking," I said.

"Just talking? At two in the morning? On your bed? Just how stupid do you think I am? This damn school is run like a zoo—girls in the boys' dorm at all hours, drugs all over the place, no discipline. It's unacceptable!"

"Oh no, Mr. Tupper, I promise that we were just talking," Katrina said, getting up and going to him, speaking in a calm, sympathetic voice. "You see, Nicholas was telling us a terribly sad story about his mother. I don't know if you know this, Mr. Tupper, but she committed suicide. Poor Nicholas found her body."

Mr. Tupper blinked several times and then tugged at his beard.

"I don't think it would be a good idea to make any sort of big whoop-de-do over this," she said. "Nicholas is very fragile, and I just think it would . . . well, I really don't know *what* might happen to him."

Mr. Tupper just looked at her.

Nicholas appeared in the bathroom doorway.

"Now I'm utterly exhausted, and you look all in yourself, Mr. Tupper. Could I ask you an enormous favor?" Katrina said, resting a palm lightly on the lapel of his bathrobe. "Would you be an absolute gentleman and escort me up to the girls' dorm? It's quite dark, and there are . . . lions and tigers and bears."

Mr. Tupper looked at each of us in turn, then muttered "spoiled rotten" under his breath and blew air through his lips. "All right, come on."

"Oh, thank you, good sir." She turned and went to Nicholas, smoothed his hair back at his temple, then leaned up and kissed his cheek. Then she came back to Mr. Tupper and slipped her arm through his.

"Blow out that candle and get to bed," Mr. Tupper told us. Then he looked down at Katrina, straightened up tall, and led her off.

8

SOMETIME IN EARLY November Nicholas got ten tabs of Sunshine acid from a friend out in Santa Cruz, and one night at dinner he suggested the four of us trip together the following Saturday. I suggested maybe one of us *not* trip in case someone had a bummer and needed to be nursed. Nicholas said bummers were a bullshit construct of the dominant culture designed to frighten wimpy suburban kids. I courageously agreed. Then Katrina said she would be my "guide" and that we'd have a delicious time. What could I say? She also suggested, with a meaningful look at me, that we invite Lenny along.

Saturday was a beautiful day, the sky blue and cloudless, the ground covered with a crazy quilt of fallen leaves; the air had that New England autumn nip, the one that triggers instant nostalgia, even in the young. I wondered if it was too late to roll around in a nice patch of poison ivy and blow up like a balloon and beg off the trip. Instead I went down to breakfast because I'd read in *Time* that taking LSD on a full stomach lessened its effect. I guess that's why my friends all skipped the meal.

I noticed Jeffrey Wilcox sitting alone, absorbed in a book, wearing an oxford shirt and a sports jacket on a Saturday. Jeffrey and I had never officially declared our shared sexuality to each other, but had tacitly acknowledged it with glances and smiles. He didn't have a lot of friends at school, and I felt sorry for him and identified with him but didn't want people to associate me with him, all of which added up to a bushel of guilt.

"Morning, Jeffrey, may I join you?"

He looked up from his book, startled.

"Oh, hi, Arthur. Sure."

I sat down and dug into my pancakes. "What are you reading?"

Jeffrey took a bookmark from the front of the book, inserted it at his page, and closed the book, his movements precise and oddly confident. "*Giovanni's Room* by James Baldwin."

"I loved that book," I said, looking him in the eye. He looked down, self-conscious about the milky spot in his pupil.

"It's wonderful . . . very sexy," he said. Then he laughed, an odd inward laugh, as if he'd said something naughty. "I live in Stamford, there's a health club in my building." He looked at me very quickly and then back down at his plate. I noticed the Volvos at the next table glancing at us with tweedy condescension. "My father's coming today."

"Oh?"

"He's taking me to see my psychiatrist. He doesn't want me to be a homosexual."

"Your father or the psychiatrist?"

"My father doesn't want me to be a homosexual. I was caught in the health club in our building, my folks were ashamed and made a big deal out of it." He blurted this out and then clapped his eyes back down to his plate. After a second he looked up to see my reaction.

I could tell Jeffrey had been traumatized by this incident, and I didn't want to add to it, so I said, "I hope it was fun."

"It was."

We smiled at each other.

"What does the psychiatrist say?"

"He wants me to say whatever comes into my mind and be uninhibited. It makes me inhibited. . . . He asks me how I feel about being homosexual."

"How do you feel?"

He stared down at the tattered remains of his pancakes. "I don't know. I just am."

His tone was matter-of-fact, with no apology, and for the first time he looked right at me. I marveled at his acceptance; he couldn't have been more than fifteen but he was way ahead of me. The truth was that while I pretended to myself that being gay was no big deal, words like *pervert*, *abnormal*, *sick* rattled around in my psyche. Plus everyone said it would ruin your prospects in life, but that didn't bother me much, I mean it wasn't like I was planning to run for Congress or play for the Yankees—in fact, being an outsider was my favorite part about being gay. All in all, the whole thing was a big ball of confusion, shame, and semen. All I really knew for sure was that I had longings for other boys and I wanted to be honest about it—both with the world and with myself.

"Do you like it here at Spooner?" I asked, to change the subject.

"It's okay," he said, looking lonely.

I knew I should spend more time with him, but he was just a kid, a kid who always had his nose in a book. I was just starting to get my head *out* of books. Besides, now that I had cool friends I didn't want to belong to the nerdy-homely-femmy club. I was a traitor to my club.

"You and Katrina are best friends, aren't you?" Jeffrey said. I nodded. "It must be nice to have a best friend like that. I never have."

That was another heartbreaker. "You will," I assured him.

"She's good for you, Arthur."

"You think so?"

"Oh yes, I've watched you. You look happier than you did before."

I was thrilled, both that I looked happier and that people could tell how close Katrina and I were. "Well, she's a wonderful friend."

"I like Miss McCoy, she gave me a book by Mary Baker Eddy."

"Mary's baker, Eddie?"

"Mary Baker Eddy," he corrected gravely.

"Is it a cookbook?"

"Oh, it's a joke. Mary's *baker* Eddie. It's a joke!" Jeffrey exclaimed, laughing, a loud sharp laugh this time, his head bobbing up and down. "A cookbook! A cookbook!" Jeffrey roared, bobbing furiously, looking like a pecking chicken. I was so happy to see him laughing. I joined in. Then he stopped. "Want to take a walk with me later?"

"You know, I can't today, I'm really sorry."

Disappointment swept over Jeffrey's face—and guilt washed over me.

"That's okay," he said.

"We'll take a walk soon, okay?"

"Yeah, sure."

"Well, I have to go," I said, wanting to get away from him—and from myself.

⁓

WE MET AT the Spot in the late morning, sat in a circle, and Nicholas handed us each this little piece of white paper smaller than my pinky nail. Filled with dread but determined to be brave, I washed it down with apple cider. For a few minutes we sat quietly, looking at each other—no turning back now—then I looked down and the ground looked like a tiny tsunami was rolling along under it.

"Arthur's tripping," Sapphire said.

"I am?" I said, looking up.

Our eyes met and we laughed, then we were all laughing—we just sat there laughing, looking at each other as our faces began shifting into Cubist Picasso heads, both eyes on one side, two noses, vast foreheads, it was funhouse mirrors without the mirrors, we laughed so hard that I could actually *see* our laughter—tiny whirling dervishes in long flinging robes, dashing madly back and forth in the air between us. It was kind of fun but *very* intense.

I lay on the ground to catch my breath—this is a *serious* drug, stay calm, stay calm—and turned to see Sapphire and Nicholas with their faces inches from a barky log.

"It's ancient Greece," Nicholas said.

"No, it's a foreign planet," Sapphire corrected.

"No, look, there's the Acropolis!"

"That's not the Acropolis, it's aliens bowling."

"It's just a log in Connecticut," Nicholas said.

Sapphire grabbed both his hands and said with infinite wisdom: "There's no such thing as *just* a log in Connecticut."

Katrina was examining a leaf—she probably thought it was the Lost City of Atlantis.

"Hi, Katrina."

"Arthur. Let's go for a walk."

As we headed off into the woods, I heard Lenny ask, "Who invented food?"

"Look," Katrina said, pointing to a large boulder covered with electric green moss. She caressed the moss, then pressed her cheek against it. "Moss is moss."

That made sense.

I leaned down and pressed my cheek against the moss.

"Mom has a house in Switzerland, the moss is my favorite thing," Katrina said.

"Swiss cheese."

"Grilled."

We sat there, cheeks to moss, like a couple of village idiots.

"Beautiful afternoon." I looked up—Mr. Spooner was standing over us, his hands clasped behind his back, a beatific Christian Science smile on his face.

My first thought, after my mind had raced up and down my body a few times, was that I was going to be expelled again, and so soon, couldn't I at least have made it until Christmas?

I desperately tried to will myself down from the acid. No luck.

I looked over at Katrina, she looked stricken, terrified—and I thought *she* was supposed to be *my* guide. I took her hand and forced myself to speak, "It *is* a beautiful afternoon, Mr. Spooner. This moss is so lovely."

"My grandmother had a moss garden," he said.

"What was it like?" I managed. Katrina was squeezing my hand so hard it hurt.

"It was at her summer place, on the Maine coast. She cut a path through the woods and cleared all the underbrush, then she put down moss, so you'd have great soaring pines with a vast carpet of moss below. It was a magical path. Grandmother used to take me on it at night. The moss glowed in the moonlight and she talked to me of elves and spirits and animals with human souls."

I wondered where Mr. Spooner had scored his acid.

"Katrina?" he said.

She crushed my hand and choked out, "Mr. Spooner?"

"How are you finding us?"

Her eyes grew absolutely round, panicky.

"Katrina loves your school," I said.

"I wish everybody did. Some people are afraid of freedom and joy, afraid to let children be children," he said, and his face tensed up, his eyes grew hard. Then he said, to himself, almost inaudibly, "I made a terrible mistake, bringing that snake into the garden." He closed his eyes and took a deep breath, his face softened. "God is love," he murmured. When he opened his eyes, they were once again light and sparkly. "Well, I must run along, dear children. Have a divine afternoon."

We watched, frozen, as he walked calmly down the path, hands clasped behind him, taking time to admire a tree here, a bird there. When he was out of sight, Katrina exhaled and threw her arms around me.

"My hero."

Acid? Bring it on.

"Sorry about my petit anxiety attack, darling, but he suddenly looked *exactly* like Norman Bates, and don't forget, the school *was* an inn. But back to reality, Noodles, you've *got* to make a play for Lenny today."

"Are you kidding?"

"No, he's tripping, his defenses are down. And believe me, he likes you, I can see it in his eyes. So kiss him, Artie, you have nothing to lose but your pride, which is an overrated virtue anyway."

Sapphire skipped into view, her face exploding with excitement, "Come on, you two, we're going to Trinculo!"

~

I COULDN'T BELIEVE that Lenny could actually drive—the road looked like an earthquake—but, jock that he was, he was sailing and smiling, swiveling around to give us a goofy grin, showing that sexy snaggle tooth. Sapphire was up front in his roomy old Mercedes, I was between Nicholas and Katrina in the back, on the radio Janis Joplin was singing about her and her Bobby McGee.

Lenny turned off the road, past two colossal stone pillars topped with leering gargoyles.

"Trinculo," Sapphire said portentously.

Suddenly the day darkened as we headed up a long drive enclosed by towering firs. The sweeping lawns on either side were overgrown with rippling grasses, in the distance I saw a formal garden, untended rose bushes in gnarly profusion, a rusty fountain topped with a winged nymph.

"It's a dream," Katrina said, drinking in the spooky splendor.

We reached an abandoned mansion, a massive Georgian affair, brick, with tall windows and columns stretching across the front— the house looked forlorn, as if it longed for company.

Inside, one huge empty room gave way to another, on and on they went, some paneled with dark wood, others trimmed with elaborate moldings, one had flocked fleur-de-lis wallpaper that looked like huge furry insects crawling up the walls. I got out of that room in a hurry.

I found myself alone in the dining room with Lenny.

"There is where Judy Drabkin puked right when we were balling," Lenny said, pointing to a spot next to a cavernous fireplace. "She was showing off how much tequila she could drink. I mean, I was like *this close* and suddenly she heaves up and pukes all over me. What a bummer." He knelt, examining the diamond-patterned parquet border. "Yeah, it was right here. See, we scratched our initials in the wood, L. S. & J. D., see? What a stupid ass thing to do, but she wouldn't ball me till we did."

I knelt beside him and examined the markings. He was wearing beat up jeans and a black T-shirt, his arms were muscular, he smelled of sweat, LSD sweat—dense, rich, faintly acrid. He was trying to grow sideburns, but they were scrawny and only looked like he'd forgotten to shave for a few days, but they did give him a swarthy working-class look. He was staring down at the floor, I was staring at him.

"Maybe a thousand years from now someone will find these and wonder what the hell they were about," he said. Then he noticed that I was staring at him and his face broke into a warm rippling smile, changing shape completely, the rugged angles dissolving into soft crinkles—his full, sensual mouth opened and that snaggle tooth appeared. Remembering Katrina's words, I leaned forward and kissed him on the lips. Me! And he didn't resist. I pressed my tongue against his teeth, they parted, his tongue touched mine.

Then the mansion reappeared.

I pulled back quickly, looking away. When I looked back, his head was cocked to the side and he seemed slightly dazed. Then he broke into that jock grin of his.

"Hey, whatever," he said.

I felt myself blush so hard it burned, but under the blush I was exultant: I had kissed Lenny! I couldn't wait to tell Katrina.

Suddenly Sapphire appeared. "Come here, you guys, we're going upstairs," she said in this ominous voice, like the Frankenstein monster was lurking up there.

As we climbed the stairs I leaned into Katrina and told her the news. She stopped and turned to me, cupped my face in her hands, "Your first kiss?" I nodded and her eyes welled with tears, which quickly gave way to a wicked pixie grin, "But not your last, Noodles, not-your-last."

Upstairs, vast rooms opened off a hallway the size of a barn. Nicholas led us into an empty echoing bedroom.

"This is where it happened," Sapphire said.

"Tell them," Lenny said with eerie anticipation.

The afternoon was aging and the light streaming through the windows was a soft pale yellow. We sat in a tight knot on the floor. Nicholas lit a cigarette, took a slow deep drag, and then opened his mouth—the smoke wafted out in a ghostly dance. "This house was built by Gregory and Lucy Battenberg at the turn of the century. They were very happy here at first, but then Audra was born. She was a beautiful baby . . . except that one of her hands was a huge, frightening, claw-like digit. They moved her into the attic, poor creature, and treated her like an idiot. Three years later Charles was born, perfect in every way—except that he adored his deformed sister, and snuck up to the attic every chance he got to play with her. Meanwhile, mom Lucy was working on a little morphine habit.

"Charles grew up, moved to New York, and married Claire Babcock, an uptight thing, and when Gregory died they moved into Trinculo. Lucy was still here and so was Audra, up in the attic. It was an unnatural arrangement because, you see, Charles still adored his sister, spent hours with her in the attic, doing who knows what, driving Claire to the edge of sanity, but her own family was stone broke. She was trapped at Trinculo. As for Lucy, she was long gone on the morphine, drifted from room to room like a ghost, a ghost who liked to lift her dress and flash her privates.

"Claire basically lived in a scotch bottle. This was her bedroom and she rarely left it, until a cousin finally convinced her to go to Silver Hill and dry out. She stayed for six weeks and returned home on March 9, 1957, in the late afternoon. The house was quiet— she climbed the stairs, sober, ready to pack her bags. She walked into *this* room. It was a tornado of food, alcohol, pills. Lucy, Audra, and Charles were on her bed together, naked. They weren't playing Scrabble. Claire went down to Charles' study, got his pistol, went into the kitchen and got a carving knife, came back up here, and blew their brains out all over these walls."

We all looked at the walls—were those faint bloodstains?

"Then she sawed off Audra's claw, put it in her purse, and drove herself back to Silver Hill. She's still there. They say the head of the place keeps the claw in a jar of formaldehyde and loves to show it off."

All was quiet and still.

Then downstairs the front door swung open with a creak that made the whole house shudder.

As one we sucked in a muffled gasp, and a fear rat scurried up my spine. We listened to the footfalls—they started up the stairs. Nicholas got up, quick, soundless, cocking his head for us to follow. In a mad silent-movie dash we made it into a closet and closed the door. Jammed together in pitch-blackness, we stood petrified and listened as the footfalls reached the top of the stairs and stopped.

I felt warm fingers on my neck, they turned my head gently, I smelled Lenny coming close and then his lips found mine, I opened my mouth and his thick tongue slid in, he boldly explored my teeth and tongue, I flicked back gently, it was so dark that I didn't know if my eyes were open or closed but I did know that my teenage soul was entering Lenny through his lips, past his snaggle tooth, and down into that place where love lives.

The footfalls grew louder, Lenny and I pulled apart with a tender reluctance. We heard muttering, the footfalls started toward the closet. The door swung open and a black man was standing there.

"Damn," he said, taking us in. He slowly broke into a huge grin, revealing a gleaming gold tooth that leaped out of the pink wet of his mouth and the rich black of his face.

"Hi, I'm Ernie."

⌒

WE SAT IN the ruined rose garden as the Connecticut evening deepened. The acid was over now and we were left empty, exhausted, needing a break from wonder. The chipped cherub in the center of the fountain looked incredibly wise, his chubby smiling face knew just what we'd been up to—behind him the horizon was a dusky orange.

Nicholas sat on a rusted cast-iron bench, absently tracing its design with his finger. Lenny sat cross-legged, tossing a pebble in the air over and over. Katrina lay on the garden's pebbled ground staring up at the sky, languidly smoking a Dunhill. I stretched out near her, our legs touching, propped up on an elbow, watching the three of them—happy, spent, among friends. Lenny and I had both been shy since our passion in the dark, which was all right with me. I found it confusing, if thrilling, and was content to let the trip wind down with quiescent grace.

Not so Sapphire.

Her orgasm's ecstatic timber came crashing down the hill toward us, causing the overgrown grass itself to undulate—the cherub's smile took on a satyr's glint. I looked up the hill at Ernie's old Buick with its lacerating fins—it was rocking with love.

By and by the car door slammed and a tousled Sapphire appeared, clutching a bottle of Jack Daniels, her beautiful black lover in tow; it had turned out that he was a quasi-caretaker for the far-flung remnants of the Battenberg clan.

"This has been a great trip," Sapphire announced, plopping down on the pebbles, her legs splayed out in front of her.

"Yeah," Ernie agreed.

9

THE NEXT MORNING I woke up feeling beyond exhausted—drained and numb and vaguely chemical. I made my way down to breakfast and found Katrina sitting alone at a corner table, looking tiny and glamorous in enormous sunglasses and a chic black coat with black-satin collar and buttons.

"How are you?" I asked.

"Ugh," she said, taking a sip of coffee. "I feel like the Jolly Green Giant picked me up and wrung me out."

"I can't believe people take that drug regularly."

"*Jamais encore.*"

We didn't talk for a while. I had none of that we're-not-talking-what-should-I-say thing I usually felt with people. Sometimes I'd lie in bed at night and imagine us over the years: When we were apart we'd write long, funny letters pouring out our souls, we'd meet up in Mexico and London and Bali, in our eighties we'd sit side by side on some porch in the Berkshires, the best of old friends.

"What are you doing for Christmas?" I asked.

"Funny you should ask, Mom called me last night to invite me out to L.A."

"That's great."

"She also mentioned some movie project, a mother-daughter thing, she said we could do a screen test together. I think that's the real reason she wants me to come. She's desperate for a gig."

"I'm sure she wants to see you."

"Hmmm, I wouldn't be so sure, Noodles, when you've been around Hollywood as long as I have you don't trust *anyone's* motives, not even your darling Mum's."

"What's Christmas like with your Mom?"

She pushed the sunglasses on top of her head—her eyes looked puffy and tired—and took out her cigarette case and lit a Dunhill. "You know, typical welfare family. One year she gave me a pony, well, actually it was a miniature horse. Our living room was the size of Grand Central Station and she had the miniature horse wrapped and I came downstairs and this huge piece of wrapping paper was dropping turds on the white carpet. There was a photographer there and Mom was freaking out but laughing to show what a good sport she was. That horse didn't make it to New Year's. I'm telling you, Artie, it's tough being a movie star's kid."

I inhaled the story and wanted more. "What about your dad?"

"Well, he's Jewish, but he's a Hollywood Jew so he sets up a huge lavish Christmas tree—and then ignores it. He always has a completely over-the-top party that centers on him sitting down at the piano and playing a little preview of his latest score. Then he calls me up to sing a carol. Which is the first time he's talked to me all night. He thinks my Mom's a moron and I inherited her brains. He hates her, just hates her."

"How come?"

"He thinks she used him. Young actress marries brilliant pillar of the Hollywood establishment, shimmies up the greasy pole, gets into A films, and dumps him for millionaire producer."

"Some moron."

"Yeah, really. Mom's father was a mailman in Wilkes-Barre, Pennsylvania. Nothing has been handed to her, I respect her for what she's accomplished. She just thinks the sun rises and sets on her hairdo. She's been okay though, she really has."

"But you don't spend a lot of time with her?"

"I saw her four times last year for a total of nineteen days. Not that I'm counting. When I was little she was out every night. She's almost forty-five now, so she's in aging-actress panic mode. Ah, Hollywood, my hometown."

In some ways it all sounded glamorous and fractured to me, but I could see how alone Katrina was. It was like she had this fabulous yacht but no mooring, no compass, no crew. Could I be some of those things for her?

She flipped her sunglasses back down. "But enough of this dreary talk, Artie, let's hitch into town. Mumsie did just send me a fat check, we'll buy a few bibelots. I've always wanted a butter churn."

10

"Darling, we've decided to go to Trinidad for Christmas. Think of it, Arthur, steel drums, all that delicious Calypso music. Sun. We'll bring piles of books. We're going to a place that has an island all to itself. Rustic, run by an English couple—for centuries, apparently. You can swim and take walks and get nut-brown and healthy," Mom said.

I stood at the pay phone in the hallway, it was just after dinner.

"Is Ann coming?"

There was a pause. I could hear her puffing her True Blue. "She's not sure yet." Mom and Ann had one of those mother/daughter-oil/water things going.

"Why not?" I said.

"Are you . . . fitting in up there, Arthur?"

"I love it here, Mom. I'm going to stay for Thanksgiving."

There was a pause and a puff. "But what will you eat?"

"Pizza."

"Oh, Arthur."

"One of my friends has invited a few of us over."

"One of the day students?"

"No, Mom, he lives in Sydney, Australia."

"Sarcasm is unbecoming in the young. What's his name?"

"His father owns a lumber mill," I said, skipping the preliminaries.

"All right, darling, if you change your mind about Thanksgiving we'll be here."

"By the way, at that Japanese restaurant, you mentioned something that you wanted Dad to discuss with me."

There was pause, she exhaled sharply, the final puff, and I pictured her grinding out the cigarette in her favorite marble ashtray. "Yes, well, I expect that discussion will take place over Christmas. Which is just as well, since it concerns both you and your sister."

"Well, can you give me a hint?"

"We're not playing charades here, Arthur. And it's really your father's place to explain things . . . Doesn't the Caribbean sound wonderful?"

Mom's abrupt changing of the subject made me realize she was uncomfortable about whatever it was Dad was going to tell us. Was it possible they were going to divorce? It didn't seem likely, they rarely fought. They did sometimes talk about moving to Europe after we kids were out of the house, could that be it? I was curious, but the truth was my life at Spooner seemed a lot more important.

"The Caribbean sounds really nice, Mom."

"We love you. Bye-bye."

I hung up and headed down to the main house to look for Katrina.

I had just stepped in the front door, when I heard—coming from upstairs—Mr. Tupper's voice raised in anger. I crept up to the top of the staircase—he was in Mr. Spooner's room. I edged closer.

"Half the kids in my class today were on drugs. It's like trying to teach zombies. Something has to be done," Mr. Tupper urged.

"I'm not going to play policeman," Mr. Spooner said calmly.

"I think a new set of rules should be instituted. These kids shouldn't even be allowed to smoke cigarettes. You need a curfew, a strict lights-out, more structured classes, mandatory attendance, weekly tests."

"My dear Mr. Tupper . . ."

"I'm not your *dear mister* anything, sir."

"Fine. My point is that I hired you to teach at *my* school. I will run it as I see fit."

"And you need some sort of physical education around here, these kids have no way to burn off their hormones. I've heard rumors of all sorts of fornicating going on, to be blunt about it."

"I don't have to sit here and listen to this," Mr. Spooner said, raising his own voice for the first time.

"All right, do things your way. But if you won't address this drug problem, I will."

"I don't appreciate being threatened."

"I don't appreciate being ridiculed by a bunch of spoiled rich kids. And I won't stand for it!"

Just then the door flew open and Mr. Tupper was on top of me—I jumped back and tried to look surprised.

"Hello, MacDougal," he said brusquely, rushing past.

I looked through the open door: Mr. Spooner was sitting at his desk, his eyes closed, his face set in firm resolve, his hands clasped in front of him—it took me a moment to realize that he was praying.

I tiptoed away.

11

LENNY CAME TO pick us up in his comfy old Mercedes on Thanksgiving afternoon. Katrina, Sapphire, and I were going. Nicholas was in Manhattan having Thanksgiving dinner at the Four Seasons, an old family tradition now in its second year.

The Solbergs lived in funky old Danbury, up on a hill overlooking the city, in a neighborhood of huge Victorians. As we pulled into the driveway, Mr. and Mrs. Solberg, both wearing worn, cozy sweaters, came out of the house to greet us. Mr. Solberg was a big gruff bear of a man with male-pattern baldness, a slab of a face that looked like it could scowl on command, and a beefy body, filling out but still fast and powerful. Mrs. Solberg looked a little like Shelly Winters, with a round emotional face and a chunky body slightly at odds with itself.

"Gobble-gobble," was the first thing out of Mr. Solberg's mouth. Mrs. Solberg laughed and pooh-poohed at the same time, then opened out her arms in a gesture of welcome. Lenny beamed at his Dad, clearly they adored each other and he was proud to be bringing his friends over.

It was a cloudy day and the red brick factories and faded row houses of Danbury stretched out below us—it reminded me of something out of a black-and-white English movie, some hardscrabble Midlands village, dreary and poetic.

"A little bubbly anyone?" Katrina asked, holding up two bottles of Dom Pérignon.

"Goodness, champagne," Mrs. Solberg said.

"Thanks for having us, Mr. and Mrs. Solberg," I said.

"I want none of this Mr. and Mrs. Solberg nonsense. I'm Nate, this is Lily. And I hope you're starving," he said, leading us into the house.

It was a classic old Victorian with high-ceilinged rooms spreading off a large entry hall—one of the front parlors had been turned into a classroom filled with tiny desks and chairs.

"Mom teaches remedial reading," Lenny explained.

Jazz was playing on the stereo as we followed Nate into the opposite parlor. There was a lazy fire going, an enormous maroon couch, mismatched easy chairs, a coffee table strewn with newspapers and magazines. A large old oil painting over the mantle—its surface cracked like broken auto glass—showed the view of Danbury from the front yard; it had hardly changed over the years.

The whole house smelled like turkey dinner.

"Make yourselves at home, who wants what to drink, et cetera, et cetera," Nate said, plopping down in an armchair and putting his feet up on the coffee table.

"Let me show them my room," Lenny said.

Nate waved his arm.. "All right, get lost."

Lily stood her ground. "I could use some help in the kitchen."

"Lily baby, I'll be right down," Sapphire said.

"Ditto *moi*," Katrina said.

"No smoking any wacky tabacky up there!" Nate called after us.

Lenny bounded up the wide central staircase—all the doors were open on the second floor and we blew past bedrooms, a music room, a study. The third floor was sanctum Lenny: three large connecting rooms that looked like a tornado had just blown through— narrow pathways wound through a shin-high explosion of clothes, toys, books, sporting equipment; the walls were a sort of time chart of Lenny's life, ranging from finger paintings with curling corners to a Jimi Hendrix poster, with blips in between marked by a dart board, egg-throwing stains, and *Playboy* centerfolds.

"My folks aren't allowed up here," Lenny said proudly.

I had no trouble believing that.

Sapphire plopped down on Lenny's mattress-on-the-floor. "Cool. Your dad is sexy."

Lenny was wearing sweat pants and a sweatshirt and I was swooning and feeling awkward. He punched me playfully in the arm. "Relax, Arthur," he said. I smiled. The place where he'd punched me throbbed slightly—I liked the feeling.

Katrina joined Sapphire on the mattress. "Lenny, I love your house, I love your parents, I love this room, it's all so divinely cozy," she said, tucking her legs under her, snuggling in.

"Let's just stay up here all day," Sapphire said.

"That wouldn't be very polite," my mom said, borrowing my vocal cords.

Sapphire absently curled a finger into Katrina's hair. I felt a pang of jealousy and sat on the mattress on the other side of Katrina.

"Katrina's agent called yesterday," Sapphire said.

"You didn't tell me," I said.

"It was just a check-in call. He always fills my ears with sweet-nothings, I don't believe a quarter of it," Katrina said—then she changed the subject. "So you've lived in this room for your whole life?" she asked Lenny, trying to grasp the concept.

"Yup. This is it. It was my mom's house since she was eleven," Lenny said, bouncing around the room with his springy energy. He grabbed a rubber ball and started tossing it against a wall, then stopped for a second and pulled off his sweatshirt. He was wearing a tight gray T-shirt, his upper body was all sinewy muscle, the T-shirt rode up on his biceps and belly as he tossed the ball, exposing more of his white flesh, flecked with faded freckles. Watching him threw me into a fit of anxiety and longing.

"Boy, things are really getting weird between Mr. Spooner and Mr. Tupper," Sapphire said.

I told them about the fight I'd overheard.

"What do you think is going to happen?" Katrina asked.

"Mr. Spooner will probably fire him," Sapphire said.

"Yeah, he fired some uptight teacher last year, either you fit or you don't at Spooner," Lenny said.

Sapphire got up and put on a Grateful Dead album and started to dance in place, tossing her head, shaking her booty like Janis Joplin. She grabbed my hand and pulled me up—I joined in, shaking my booty like a goose with arthritis.

None of us talked for a while, Lenny tossed the ball, Sapphire and I danced, Katrina sat on the mattress and smoked—it felt very beatnik, very existential, not that I knew what the word meant, but I'd seen a picture of Jean-Paul Sartre in some magazine and he looked incredibly deep and weird and romantic in an anguished sort of way. It was like the four of us were solitary universes grooving on the meaninglessness of being teenagers. Something like that. It was all very anti-Thanksgiving. The song ended, we all sensed the same vibe, we were all in the same Antonioni movie, the Lost Generation, Lenny's ball-throwing our rubbery pulse.

At least until Sapphire's stomach grumbled.

"Guess I'll go down and help Lily with dinner," she said with a grin.

"Me too, I'm brilliant at opening cans," Katrina said, giving me a meaningful glance that included an encouraging nod in Lenny's direction.

SUDDENLY I WAS alone with Lenny. I became queasy. Our acid kisses had never been mentioned. I remembered them, the taste of his mouth, the smell of his sweat. They became a presence in the room—it was me, Lenny, and our kisses. He kept tossing the ball against the wall, seemed to grow a little overly casual. I walked to the window and sat on the sill, wishing I'd gone downstairs, wishing I was anywhere but where I was.

The November sun was starting to sink and the light in the room took on a dense gray quality, a neighbor was burning leaves and the smell drifted in the window. Down the hill, in the houses of Danbury, lights were being turned on and the distant rooms looked snug and warm, as if small, comfortable lives were being lived there. I wanted to live in safe little rooms like that, busy with small domestic chores, away from the pull of my fevered needs and the confusion of my future.

"So, man . . ." Lenny said.

I turned—he was sprawled on his mattress, his legs spread, his arms up behind his head: Was this an invitation? My stomach did a back flip. I looked away, wishing I could disappear, but the image of his body stayed in my mind, the fullness at the crotch of his sweat-pants. Involuntarily I looked back, my eyes went to that place, a wave of desire swelled through me.

"Should we go downstairs?" I stammered, sweat trickling down my rib cage.

"You're blushing."

"I am?"

I'd worked up my courage to the point where I could look at Lenny for a split second, concentrating all my energy on not glanc-ing between his legs. He was smiling a warm it's-okay-Arthur smile.

"You like guys, huh?"

"Yeah," I managed. I turned and looked down at Danbury—more lights had come on in the little houses.

"It's okay, Arthur, it's no big deal." He got up and crossed to me, mussed my hair, his fingers felt strong. I looked at him—his eyes were filled with kindness.

"No big deal," I said bitterly. I walked over to the cluttered man-tle, needing to get away from him. There was a matchbox toy, a tiny truck, buried in the jumble. I picked it up.

"You want to fool around?" Lenny said in a low, inviting voice.

I wasn't sure which scared me more, declining or accepting. "With you?"

"No, with Mamie Eisenhower."

"She's not my type."

"Too old?"

"Nah, I'm just not into flowered dresses."

"Come here, man."

I turned—he was back on the mattress, propped up on an elbow, rubbing his lower belly, where hair curled up from below. I walked over to the bed, the matchbox truck in my hand, lay down next to him, and ran the little truck up his arm.

"Tickles."

"It does?"

"A little. Feels good."

"You're nice, Lenny."

We were talking in whispers—pale-orange tinted the gray light coming in the window, the room felt very still.

"You like being here?"

"Yeah."

"It's nice, isn't it?"

"Yeah."

Without thinking I touched his hand, his forearm was covered with long reddish-brown hairs, I ran my fingertips gently over the hairs, goosebumps broke out on his skin, he smiled at me.

"Do you remember when we kissed?" I asked. As soon as the words were out I felt lighter. Lenny nodded. "Did you like it?"

"Yeah, I did."

"You mostly like girls, don't you?" I ran my finger along his neck, tracing the collar of his T-shirt.

"I like you."

I ran my thumb down his sideburn and cheek. "You've fooled around before?"

"Oh yeah. At camp. With my cousin once. It's no big deal. I like girls. But you know, it's all . . . life. Or something."

Then I hugged him. He returned the hug. I was instantly hard, tightening my grip, kissing him, surprised by my own ardor, both lost in sensation and recording our every move.

⁓

"Gooble, gobble! Come and get it, boys! It's turkey time!"
Nate's voice boomed up from the second floor landing.

Lenny and I grinned at each other.

"Be right down, Dad," he yelled as he got up and hunted for
something to wipe us up with.

The food looked amazing but I had no appetite, my body was so
content, filled with such a delicious liquid warmth. We hadn't even
done all that much, just a lot of touching and kissing and rubbing,
but it had been enough—I had entered the magical realm of sex,
and, as Lily led us in grace, it wasn't the food I was giving thanks for.

12

I WAS SITTING in the library one cold Saturday afternoon in mid-December, finishing off my applications to second- and third-tier colleges in Los Angeles and San Francisco. California held a shimmering, mythical allure for me—Sunset Boulevard, Spanish missions, Sam Spade, bohemian poets, the nascent gay liberation movement—it all filled me with a promise and yearning so intense that it almost hurt. But getting the applications done was nothing but drudgework, so I was delighted when Katrina interrupted me.

"Artie, want to come to town with me? I'm going to buy Mumsie some X-mas presents."

"I should really finish off at least one of these college applications."

Katrina yawned.

"Oh, all right, you talked me into it," I said.

We decided to walk the two miles into Westridge. It was a clear day suffused with that sharp winter light that throws everything into crystalline relief. The road to town wound past open fields, stone walls, and large old houses. Katrina looked very tomboyish in jeans rolled up at the bottom and a barn coat. She was in high spirits, walking with her bouncy step.

"Mom called last night, she's got all sorts of stuff planned for the holidays," she said excitedly, turning to face me, walking backwards.

"Like what?"

"She's rented a yacht for a day trip out to Catalina, we're going to a party up in Santa Barbara, and a Christmas concert at the new Music Center downtown."

"Wow," I said, wishing she'd invite me along. "Will you see much of your Dad?"

"I called to tell him I was coming last week, left a message with his assistant, and I still haven't heard back. I'm sure I'll go to his annual bash and do my singing doll routine."

I wanted to ask about the boy she'd been involved with, but decided it might ruin her mood.

"Have you heard anything more about that screen test you and your mom were going to do?"

"No, but I'm having lunch with Kander and Ebb in New York, on my way to L.A."

"Boy, that's exciting! How come you never tell me these things?"

"Oh, I don't want to seem braggadocios, I guess." She ran her fingers through her hair and shook her head. "Artie, look!"

She pointed across the field beside us, to a large brown horse. The horse saw us and trotted over. Katrina petted his long face. The animal's eyes grew lidded in appreciation. "Oh, what a sweet, beautiful baby."

I admired horses—from a distance. A few years earlier, Mom—in one of her periodic efforts to get me engaged in "stimulating activities"—had signed me up for riding lessons at the Claremont Stables on West Eighty-ninth Street. After three lessons with a grand, seedy old Austrian gentleman, I was encouraged to take my horse out on a ride through Central Park. About five minutes into the park, as we neared the Tavern on the Green, the horse reared up, dumped me on the ground, and raced away. I walked back to the stable, humiliated and worried about the horse. When I arrived he was happily chewing hay, and shot me a dismissive look. I never went back.

Katrina was climbing the fence.

"What are you doing?"

"I'm going to go for a ride."

"Bareback?"

"*Bien sur.*"

"Do you know how to ride?"

"No, but I'll catch on."

She was on top of the fence, getting ready to slip onto the horse's back. I reached up and wrapped my arms around her waist and pulled. We struggled, but I was stronger and I got her down. She turned, my arms still around her—we were face-to-face, close, I could feel her breath on my cheek.

Katrina whispered, "You really care about me, don't you, Artie?"

"You could have gotten hurt."

She looked up at me, her eyes grew soft. She slowly leaned in toward me, as if she were going to kiss me, then she turned her head and rested it on my chest. "Thank you for watching over me."

Our intimacy, her need, scared me—did she want us to be lovers? The horse whinnied for attention. I jammed my hands in my pockets, took a step backwards.

Katrina looked startled for a moment. Then she turned to the horse and gently petted its nose. "Carry on, brave creature." She threw back her shoulders and shook her head. "Come on, Artie, let's hustle."

Westridge was decked out in its Christmas finery, with evergreens and holly filling the window boxes and planters, and lights twinkling in the shop windows. It looked like the miniature village of my old model train set. Katrina led me into an antique shop. The place was sparse and spotless, and the proprietor was a youngish blond woman wearing a Christmas sweater and a black velvet headband.

"Hi, there," she chirped. She studied Katrina for a moment, before saying, with a sly grin, "I know you."

Katrina's eyes widened. "You do?"

"*Look* magazine, two years ago: 'Christmas with Jean Clarke.' You were so adorable making that snowman."

"Oh God, haunted by the sins of my past. Actually a prop man from Paramount made the snowman. But the snow was real—well, it was real fake snow. Mom covered the whole backyard with it. Most depressing sight of my life."

"May I ask what you're doing in Westridge?"

"Artie and I go to school here. At Spooner."

The woman's face darkened for a mini-instant, before she recovered with a big smile. "So, are you looking for anything in particular?"

"I'm looking for some acutely New England presents to bring home for *this* year's Christmas with Jean Clarke."

The woman could barely contain her excitement, and she led us through the store making suggestions and detailing the provenance of every portrait and painted chest. Katrina ended up buying a folk art whirligig, a small hooked rug, and some cans of Indian pudding.

"Mummy will *love* these things," Katrina said with touching enthu-siasm. "Can you ship them out to Los Angeles for me?" She reached into her bag, searched around for a moment, and pulled out a crumpled pile of cash.

"Of course." The woman grew serious. "You know, I think your mother is really an extraordinary actress. She's so full of life and passion, she makes *me* feel alive. I was very moved by her perfor-mance in *The Web We Weave.*"

Katrina was still for a moment, her wit silenced—I sensed that hearing how her mother's gifts had affected this woman unsettled her in some way that she couldn't easily dismiss.

"**LET'S STOP FOR** a cup of java," Katrina said when we were back outside.

We went into Westridge's luncheonette—a homey place with pink vinyl booths and a matching counter that looked like it belonged in a real town. We sat at the counter.

"This place is so *authentique*, it *demands* lemon meringue pie," Katrina said, curling her legs around each other and lighting a cigarette.

The waitress took our pie and coffee order.

"Katrina?"

She looked at me expectantly.

"What's it like having strangers stake a claim on you like that?"

She took a deep pull on her cigarette and blew the smoke sky-ward. "Well, it's not as if *I've* done anything to earn it, it's all reflected glory, isn't it? So, I suppose it makes me feel lucky . . . and guilty and . . ." A lost look swept over her, then she raked her fingers through her hair and shook her head. "Oh, darling, let's not play shrink, it's Christmas."

The pie came but she seemed to have lost interest and only picked at a corner of meringue with her fingers. Then she looked around the restaurant, turned to me, and said *sotto voce*, "Check out the back booth."

I turned—Mr. Tupper and four other faculty members, none Scientists, were huddled in the booth, deep in conversation. A cloud of cigarette smoke hung over them, and Mr. Tupper was gripping the edge of the table with both hands, leaning forward, speaking intently.

"Boy, they really look like they're plotting something," I said.

"Mutiny on the Spooner," Katrina said, cheering up, taking an enormous bite of pie with one hand as her cigarette still burned in the other.

13

A BIG CHRISTMAS party was planned to send us all off filled with good cheer and school spirit. School had that last-day-before-vacation feel to it that Friday, classes were relaxed, attendance even spottier than usual, anticipation crackled in the air. I found Katrina in the library, lying on the bench with her head buried in *Villette*, a six-hundred-page book by Charlotte Brontë.

"A little light reading?" I said, sitting on the floor next to her.

"Oh, Artie, I'm just pretending to read this, it's way too dense for me, might as well be written in Arabic." She closed the book and sat up, cross-legged.

"So what time are you leaving for Los Angeles tomorrow?"

"I'm not going," she said casually.

"What? Why not?"

"I just decided not to go."

"Just like that?"

"Ar*thur*, it's no big deal," she said, lifting up the book and saying, eyes on the page, "I'm staying here."

"Here? At Spooner?"

She nodded.

"By yourself. For two weeks?"

"No doubt I'll pop into New York for a *soiree* or two."

"Katrina, what happened?"

"You know, Arthur, sometimes you ask too many questions."

I felt a stab of rejection and hurt. I got up and made a great show of browsing through the shelves. Katrina lay back down on the bench with *Villette*.

"Mother's secretary called this morning to tell me she's unexpectedly gone to Gstaad for the holidays with some man I've never heard of," she said flatly. "As for my father, let's just say we're not speaking at the moment."

I felt another stab of hurt, but this time it was her hurt, and it was a much sharper stab. I went and lay on the floor beside the bench, put my hands behind my head and looked up at the brass chandelier, spindly and defunct. Out of the corner of my eye I saw Katrina rest the book on her chest.

"I'll stay with you."

"No."

"Why not? It'll be fun, you can sleep in Nicky's bed and we can read and listen to records and take walks. It'll be spooky and fabulous."

"What about your family?"

"Who cares? I'd much rather be with you than stuck on some sun-baked island with them."

Katrina didn't say anything but I could tell she liked the plan.

"I'm going to go call right now."

⌒

"ARTHUR, THAT IS the most absurd idea since Bucky Fuller wanted to put a dome over Manhattan! Spend Christmas at that deserted school with that strange child? After we've gone to no small trouble, not to mention expense, to plan a lovely family vacation at this smashing little place. Out of question. I forbid it," Mom said, pulling out all the stops.

As always when my mother slipped into her dominatrix mode, I shrank in response, felt utterly powerless, could feel frustration shooting through my body like a drug.

She switched gears to soften me up for the kill. "Listen, darling, it'll be a lovely time. There'll be swimming and snorkeling, you adore snorkeling, coral and colors and tropical fish. Now let's be grownups about this."

I knew she had a point about the plans and the expense, but it made me angry that I knew she had a point, and that she was able—not to mention willing—to emasculate me so easily. I also knew, as I heard her light a True Blue, that I would be going to the Caribbean for Christmas.

"Are you there, Arthur?'

"Yeah," I grunted.

"So we'll see you tomorrow then?" she said, treading lightly.

"Yeah."

"Wonderful, darling. We've got tickets to *Hair*, some wild new show full of naked hippies. Sounds like great fun. Then Sunday we're off for Calypso land," she said, the whole little unpleasantness behind her.

I hung up feeling hollow and tiny.

***

WHEN I WALKED back into the library Katrina was still lying there with *Villette*. She looked at me over the top of the book, hopeful.

"I guess I'm going."

She gave a heartbreaking little shrug and went back to her not-reading. I felt like the worst friend who ever lived. I walked over to the window and looked out at the campus—kids were milling around in the sunshine, smiling and happy. It all looked so far away.

"It's all right, Artie." She sat up on the bench.

"Won't you be lonely?"

"It won't be the first time. I've gotten pretty good at amusing myself, really . . . Listen, Arthur, don't tell anyone I'm going to be staying."

"Why not?" I asked, but as soon as the words were out of my mouth I wished I could suck them back in.

"Just because," she said, lying back down and burying her nose in the book.

14

NICHOLAS HAD A bottle of red wine and we sat on my bed with the lights out, drinking from little paper cups and watching out the window as the party got underway down at the main house; the sounds of the Rolling Stones drifted up to us.

"Move over, Truman Capote, *this* is the party of the decade," Nicholas said.

The florid and blowsy Mrs. Markum, the girls' dorm mother, wobbled tipsily toward the front door wearing a rhinestone-covered hot pink evening gown that hugged every bulge; in her hair she'd stuck what looked like a bright red feather duster. She tripped on the front step and we could see her mouth say "Shit!" before she regained her composure and made her entrance.

"Well, Arthur, we made it to Christmas."

"Yes, we did."

"What do you think of the old Spooner School?" The boys' dorm felt empty, that bittersweet everybody-just-left empty. "It's okay, isn't it?" If I hadn't known him better I would have sworn he was a little choked up.

"It is okay, more than okay."

"Let's raise a glass to the soon-to-be alma mater," he said, refilling our cups. We brought them together with a waxy clink and drank.

"We'll all stay in touch next year, don't you think?" I said.

"Yeah sure, we'll all get a house together in Vermont and have our own little hippie commune. I'll milk the goats, you can play the dulcimer, Katrina can do macramé, and Sapphire will bake the hash brownies." I was hurt by his sarcasm and I guess it showed, because he leaned back against the wall and closed his eyes. "I'm sorry, I really am an asshole."

"It's okay."

"No, it's not okay. It's fucked up. I'm fucked up." We were silent for a moment. "Look, Arthur, who knows if we'll even be alive next year, or if the planet will still be here. It's not past those jokers to nuke Hanoi, you know."

I nodded, wishing I hadn't exposed myself in the first place. "Guess I should head down to the party."

"Wait," Nicholas said with sudden intensity. "Let's have one more glass of wine first," he added, too casually, covering his tracks. He was spooked, no doubt.

"Okay."

We drank in silence. A bright red car drove up, a European car, compact and classy. Sophia and Cutter Newcomb got out—she was wearing a shawl, which she hugged around her, he had on an overcoat with a beaver collar, like he was going to the Harvard-Yale game. Head held high, she walked ahead of him, he straightened up with feigned sobriety—you could almost see the chasm between them. There was something so sad about this soulful, vibrant woman married to this pickled Ivy League caricature. Why didn't she just walk away, find some man who could see how amazing she was, who could bring joy to her beautiful weary face?

"What will your Christmas be like?" I asked Nicholas.

"Lyford Cay, a house that looks like a hotel, servants in white jackets lurking in all the corners, I feel like I'm a visitor in *their* house. Daddy will bring along his latest girlfriend, chickadee, baby-doll, who will be excruciatingly nice to me even though she doesn't know whether to play big sister or—please-dear-God-don't-let-it-happen—stepmother. What they don't know—sweet, almost-bright young things—is that Daddy is a ball 'em and boot 'em type of guy. Bye-bye birdie, here's a little trinket from Tiffany to grease your slide. I tend to have my first rum cooler with breakfast. Christmas in bathing trunks is so surreal."

"I guess I'll find out," I said, already missing the festive hubbub and movie-going orgy of my Manhattan Christmases.

Nicholas got up, crossed to his own bed and fell onto it.

"Oh, Arthur," he said wearily.

I knew how he felt, but the Beatles were playing, the party beckoned.

"I'm going to head down," I said, and left without waiting for an answer.

A cold front had swept down from Canada and the cloudless night was bracing, the stars that leaped out of the black moonless sky were honed to pinpoint radiance. Being outdoors filled me with the thrill of freedom, my shoulders spread and my breath came easier. Down the hill windows blazed, music played. Out here, in the night, I was alone with myself, and for a moment the world seemed a place throbbing with possibility, a labyrinth of fascinations, a carnival of artists and lovers—and the future a place I might want to visit.

"Arthur!"

I turned to see Sapphire running down the hill from the girls' dorm in full Janis regalia—a blur of fringe, feathers, and bangles, a ratty old raccoon coat flying out behind her—grinning madly, excited, her eyes tossing friendship at me. She greeted me with a gut-busting hug that felt good and warm and female, she smelled like a vat of patchouli oil, her eyes were lined with thick black eyeliner, and she was wearing a leather headband with a scarab that smushed down the crown of her hair, below it her mane burst out in curly defiance. I was overcome with affection for her—she was so Sapphire.

"You look beautiful," I said.

"Thanks, cutie."

"Where's Katrina?"

"Still up in our room, getting ready, I think she wants to make an entrance."

"She's all right, isn't she?"

"She's working her way through a bottle of Dom Pérignon and she took some kind of pill, an upper I think. Did something happen, did she get some bad news?"

"Not that I know of."

"Don't tell me—Nicholas is being a piggy bore, lying on his bed and moping about how meaningless life is. He does it every Christmas, I've stopped playing Mommy." She hooked her arm in mine. "Shall we, darling?"

"Let's."

Lenny, groovy in a bowling shirt and tight black pants, had set up a DJ table and was playing Jefferson Airplane; the dance floor was filled with kids and a few game teachers. In spite of the dancers the mood was strained in extremis: the Christian Science crowd was sitting, wagons circled, on one side of the room, while Mr. Tupper, dressed like Santa Claus, was holding forth on the other, regaling his audience, acting as if it was his party, his school.

Sapphire made a beeline for the dance floor and I headed over to the food table, hoping to avoid my teachers. I'd always had this weird guilt thing about seeing teachers outside the classroom; I was sure they could just look at me and know that I'd taken every possible shortcut, usually including cheating, to get a passing grade. In fact, I often put in more time preparing to cheat—writing whole paragraphs from textbooks in minute script on the inside of my wrist, for example—than I would have had to put into studying in order to pass. I guess it was the principal of the thing.

"Merry Christmas, Arthur," Mr. Spooner said, appearing out of nowhere.

"Merry Christmas, Mr. Spooner."

He was smiling, but there was no hiding the tension behind it. "Looking forward to your holiday?"

"Yes."

"Plans?"

"We're going down to the Caribbean, to a little island off Trinidad."

"Should be fascinating, the history, the topography, the culture."

"Yes, I expect it will be."

This was just the kind of conversation that freaked me out: we weren't talking about what was really going on, which was that he was fighting with Mr. Tupper for control of his school, my best friend was in bad shape, I was gay, he probably was too, and the world was a greed-driven shithole instead of the Garden of Eden it could be.

"I remember the first time I saw this campus, it was a rainy day in late June, it was a warm rain, life-giving. I knew as I came up the drive, I knew it was right, the right place for my school. I *felt* it." He got that dreamy look on his face.

"It's a nice school, Mr. Spooner."

"I'm so glad that you're with us."

I grabbed a piece of turkey and some mashed potatoes and headed to an out-of-the-way chair. I had just sat down when Katrina blew in, looking very mod in a red mini-dress, matching heels, and red ball earrings—all eyes went to her. "Artie, darling!" she cried, rushing over to me.

She was flying high.

"Are you hungry?"

"Oh, Artie," she said dismissively, looking around nervously with small jerking motions of her head.

"Come on, ya big boozer, let's boogie," Sapphire said, barreling over, grabbing Katrina's hand and pulling her onto the dance floor.

Junior Walker and the All-Stars were playing and they began to dance. Their styles were a study in contrasts—Sapphire was all over the place, *in* the music, shaking with wild abandon, Katrina was performing, all easy grace and sure rhythm, doing deft little moves, riding the music, smooth.

Lenny caught my eye and gestured me over to the DJ table. Our escapade at Thanksgiving hadn't been repeated. I would have loved to, but I could tell he was shy about it, when we were alone he tensed up, and I had the feeling that for all the fooling around he claimed he'd done, he'd never gotten quite as into it as he had with me. I certainly didn't want to force things; besides those luscious moments up in his room continued to pay dividends—why, I relived them practically every day.

"Hey, chowdahead," Lenny said, loose in the safety of the party, throwing an arm over my shoulder and pulling me to him—I smelled alcohol on his breath. The Stet feel of his muscular body gave me an instant semi-stiffy.

"Hey, sexy," I said.

"I'm trying to get this party going."

"It's going all right."

"Come on," he said, pulling me after him, leading me to a back hallway that led to the kitchen—it was darker back there and smelled like cafeteria food and damp mops. He leaned his shoulders against the wall, pushed his hips forward. "So how the hell are you?" he asked with a sly grin.

"I'm okay, I guess."

"You look a little bummed." He pulled a flask out of his back pocket and took a deep slug and then held it out to me. "This might help."

I took the flash and held it under my nose: scotch. Ugh, I *hated* scotch.

"Go ahead," he said. The music was pounding in the background and he put a hand on the back of my neck. "Drink it." I liked the way it felt when he forced my head down like that. I took a drink and it burned, but within seconds my belly felt warm and I relaxed a little.

"Good boy," he said. Then he looked down his body. I followed his eyes, to the bulge at his crotch—it grew larger, more delineated. "You want that, don't you?"

My throat went dry and I nodded my head. I leaned in to kiss him.

"No kissing."

He was acting so differently from Thanksgiving, there was no affection, just a taunting masculine sexuality. More confusion. I had furtively read *City of Night* at the library, I knew about rough trade, role playing, all that, but my fantasies of gay love ran more toward some soft-focus image of two equals—sensitive, long-limbed young men taking walks across the bucolic English countryside before retreating to a sweet enfolding room up under the eaves for a long afternoon of lovemaking, passionate but playful, the soft waning sunlight time's only intrusion on their idyll.

But if Lenny saw things differently, well, who was I to argue? I certainly couldn't argue with the want that was making my knees go soft.

"Get in there," he said, cocking his head in the direction of a dark pantry.

I turned and he grabbed my hips and pushed himself against my rear end—*ooohhh*.

The pantry was long and narrow and I went to the far end— Lenny stood in the doorway, his body silhouetted against the frame. "Kneel down," he said, his voice thick, hushed. I did. He came toward me slowly and stopped. I looked up at him. He reached down, put a warm strong hand on either side of my head and tilted it down so that my eyes were level with his crotch—his dick was straining against the material. He rubbed my cheek with one hand, gentle, encouraging, with the other he reached for his zipper.

The music stopped.

There was silence—as if the whole party was frozen in mid-beat—and then a growing chorus of "Where's Lenny?"

"Shit," he muttered. He reached down under my arms and pulled

me to my feet. In the dim light his eyes were twinkling with lascivi-
ous warmth. "That was fun."

"I'll say," I managed, feeling like I was on a roller coaster that had
suddenly stopped at the lip of a steep drop—my stomach hollow, my
breath shallow.

"All right, one kiss." He leaned in and put his lips on mine, I
pushed out my tongue but he wouldn't open his mouth—then he
did, for just a second, and our tongues touched. Then he pulled
away and hopped around a bit, reaching down into his pants and
rearranging himself.

He disappeared, but I was too excited to leave things hanging. I
went out the kitchen's back door, found a dark spot behind a bush,
and finished the job—and the images that flashed in my head weren't
of playful passion under the eaves.

I WALKED BACK into the party to find Sapphire and Katrina the
stars of the show, dancing to *Proud Mary* with the party gathered
around them, cheering them on. Sapphire threw her arms over her
head and limboed down on bent knees—Katrina mimicked her and
the crowd howled. Katrina slithered across the floor in a rock 'n'
roll flamenco, one hand held against her stomach, the other cradling
an imaginary partner—Sapphire copied this to more howls. It was a
duel of the dance moves and the two girls were wild, elated, loving
every bit of the attention.

Suddenly Mrs. Markum, sloshed to the gills, burst through the
circle and started to boogie along: It's *my* party too, goddamnit!
One shoulder seam of her evening gown had popped, the feather
duster in her hair was all akimbo, and the mascara on her left eye

had been rubbed and smudged into a huge black shiner, but that
didn't stop her from tossing her head and throwing up her arms like
some sexy 1940s movie star.

Sapphire made an "I'm exhausted" gesture and left the dance
floor. But Katrina didn't—she turned to Mrs. Markum and began
to match *her* move for move. The party broke into spontaneous
applause. Katrina danced harder, pushing herself, her face glistening with sweat—her grace had given way to effort, but she didn't
want to surrender the spotlight, to disappoint the crowd. Was I the
only one to see desperation in her eyes?

I went to the DJ table. "Lenny," I said, raising my voice over the
music.

"Yeah?" he said with a wide grin.

"Play something slow next."

"Oh, come on, this thing is just starting to swing."

"Please, Lenny, play something slow, *please.*"

Lenny shrugged "okay." I pulled him away from the table and
leaned into his ear, "Listen, Katrina is going to be on campus over
the holiday, but she doesn't want anyone to know it. Will you come
over and check on her, please?"

"Sure, man."

"But don't make it look like that's what you're doing, okay?
Really. Pretend you forgot something on campus, tell her some
story, act surprised when you see her. *Promise?*"

"Okay, Arthur."

"Maybe you could invite her over for dinner or something."

"I'll do that."

The song ended and Lenny put on *Try a Little Tenderness*. The circle
broke up and I saw Katrina standing there, alone, dazed, panting.
I went to her. No one was dancing, everyone was watching her,

watching us. She looked at me, unfocused for a moment, sweat pouring off of her.

"May I have this dance?" I asked.

"I shouldn't have done that," she said, and her face went slack, melted into a terrible sadness.

"No, Katrina, it was wonderful."

"You don't understand, I used to do that at my parents' parties, carry on like that, with everyone egging me on, pretty little Katrina, the dancing doll. I don't feel well, I want to go to bed, I want to be alone."

"Can I walk you up to the dorm?"

"I'd rather you didn't." She reached up and touched my cheek and gave me a weary, almost pitying look, as if I was very sweet but utterly clueless. "Darling Artie." Then she raked her fingers through her hair, shook her head, threw back her shoulders, and, looking straight ahead, walked across the room and out into the night.

15

THE NEXT MORNING I went looking for Katrina, to say good-bye and make sure she was okay.

It was a rainy, chill December morning and the boys' dorm was clearing out quickly; as I dressed I heard doors slamming and *see-you-next-years* exchanged. Nicholas' dad was sending a car up for him and I was going to hitch a ride.

I put on an old yellow slicker that I'd had since I was twelve and headed outside. The rain was a gray film, the earth smelled wet and barky, clumps of soggy leaves gathered against the stone walls, the world felt empty and closed in, the rain pinged off my slicker, I felt cold and I liked it. Katrina wasn't in the dining room so I walked down to the lake—its surface was alive with dancing raindrops and the wet of the earth and air seemed to merge with the lake, enclosing me in a watery dream.

Across the lake, Katrina materialized out of the vapors. She stood on the shore and held her head up to the drops. As I walked around the lake toward her, she knelt down and cupped her hands in the water, bringing them up full. She watched the rain bounce in the tiny lake in her palms.

"Katrina," I said, reaching her. She looked about eleven years old in jeans, a sweatshirt, and a boy's team jacket, all soaked.

"Hi, Arthur," she said without looking up.

I stood over her, she opened her hands and the lake sluiced out. She looked up at me—her hair was plastered down, her skin was drawn tight over her bones, her eyes exhausted.

"Did you get any sleep?" I asked.

"Not much."

"Well, you look really tired. Are you going to be all right here alone?"

"What are you—my mother?"

There was a pause. She gave a strangled little laugh.

"Isn't that the problem?" I said.

I realized that we were talking very loudly because of the rain, almost shouting, and it made everything we said seem urgent.

"Why don't you mind your own fucking business?" she said, and gave me a withering look.

Hot tears welled up inside me. I turned and walked away.

"Arthur," she called. She caught up with me and turned me around. The rain was coming down harder; I looked at her through the gray curtain of water.

"I'm sorry," she said. Her head was tilted slightly and she was blinking through the raindrops—or were those tears? She looked so beautiful and so lost.

"That's okay," I said.

We looked at each other.

"Aren't you freezing?" I asked.

She nodded.

We ducked into the nearest doorway, the theater studio. The large room had a concrete floor painted gray and windows that faced the lake, it felt dank and cellar-like, smelled like wet cement.

Katrina started to shiver; she took off the jacket. I went into the bathroom and found a roll of paper towels. I scrubbed her hair with wads of them, the paper clumped and shredded, I went through practically the whole roll before her hair was half dry.

She took off her soaking sweatshirt and was naked underneath; there were goosebumps on her white skin. I slipped off my slicker, took off my wool shirt, and held it open for her—she slipped into it and I briskly rubbed her arms and back. She kicked off her sneakers and peeled off her soggy jeans, I pulled off my shoes and wet jeans. I was in my socks and jockey shorts, Katrina was in her panties and my wool shirt. We didn't talk.

Outside the window the world was a gray mist, the only sound the patter of the rain. There was a record player in the corner. Katrina turned it on and leafed through the records until she found one she liked. Billie Holiday's voice filled the room—*In My Solitude*.

We took each other in our arms and started to dance.

16

THE SENSATION OF getting on a plane in freezing gray New York and stepping off in the blazing pastel tropics three hours later gave me some idea of how Dorothy must have felt when she landed in Oz—the warm air hit like a wind tunnel and I could feel my muscles relax with the force of a thousand Miltowns.

"The infant mortality rate is staggering," my sister said as our taxi wound its way through the streets of Port of Spain. Ann was in her sophomore year at Antioch—she lived in sandals, was a vegetarian, and wore a perpetually indignant expression brought on by her acute identification with the suffering masses of the Third World. Still a virgin, she adored Dad and had a not-very-well-repressed rage toward Mom, which took the form of her bursting into tears and rushing off to her room to sulk whenever Mom made a snobbish remark about the working classes.

I found Ann hopelessly sincere and earnest—she wouldn't get a joke if it ran her over—but she was my big sister and I loved her and worried about her and felt sorry for her. And I prayed she hadn't packed any of her wooly Mexican ponchos, they were so embarrassing; she was absentminded and not very practical—she'd packed her one-piece black bathing suit on our last ski trip—so I wouldn't put it past her.

"I've been reading all about the history of Trinidad, it's unbearably unjust, these people have been shamelessly exploited. Oh God, it makes me angry!" she moaned.

I looked out the window of the old Ford, which smelled like hot car-seat vinyl—the deep-black Trinidadians looked vibrant and relaxed, calypso drifted from a café radio. "They look pretty happy to me."

"Arthur, you just don't understand," Ann said in exasperation. Mom lit a cigarette. "Mommy, do you know how much tobacco pickers are paid?"

"They do look happy, Charles," Mom said, ignoring her daughter.

Ann, who was sitting between me and Mom in the back seat, leaned forward and put her elbows on her knees; she was wearing men's khaki shorts and didn't shave her legs, which I found almost as embarrassing as the ponchos—Mom found it more so. "Daddy, they just don't understand. It's so utterly simplistic to look out a taxi window and say 'They look happy.' These people aren't educated, they don't *know* how exploited they've been. If they knew, they'd be miserable," she said, looking far more miserable than any of the exploited Trinidadians.

"I won't have this vacation spoiled by a lot of your silly, and I might add frightfully simplistic, theories," Mom said. "I want everyone to be pleasant for the next ten days, and please do not try to become best friends with the help, Ann, it's very unbecoming."

Three summers earlier, when we'd rented a house on Mykonos, Ann had dragged an ancient peasant couple home for dinner. They looked like wizened potatoes, had dirt deep in their pores, spoke not a word of English, and sat there staring at Mom's *salade niçoise* like it had been cursed by the devil. Mom clammed up, and poor Ann was forced to plow through the meal using a Greek-English phrase book to bring out the couple on the subject of rich Americans destroying the fragile social structure of the Greek Isles.

We arrived at the wharf, where a launch was waiting to ferry us over to the hotel. I thought of Katrina as I watched Trinidad recede, growing smaller and smaller until the sky and water met and it disappeared.

The hotel was the only thing on the small, scruffy island. It was a rambling old affair, rundown in a casual, WASPy way, the common rooms filled with books, games, and card tables, the bedrooms white and almost austere, the endless veranda lined with weathered wicker. It attracted a lot of old couples from places like Blue Hill, Maine and Dorset, Vermont, very less-is-more-even-though-we-have-lots types who mostly read and slept and drank—I noticed that many spent all day with a drink by their side. The place, which Mom immediately dubbed "a dinosaur's playground," was run by a sun-baked old English couple who talked very slowly and seemed perpetually half-sloshed themselves.

I spent my days taking long walks around the island, climbing on the old World War II battlements, and tossing food to the beautiful lizards. After about three days I got bored and took up compulsive masturbation. I called the Spooner campus every day from the hotel's one phone booth—an elaborate procedure involving two operators and long waits—but there was never an answer. Finally I called Lenny.

"Hi, man," he said.

"Have you seen Katrina?"

"I went over there the other day and couldn't find her."

"Did you try the girls' dorm?"

"Arthur, I'm more than just a piece of meat, I have a brain you know."

"I'm sorry, Lenny, it's just that I'm worried about her."

"Well, I really don't think she's anywhere on campus, I checked all over."

"Thanks, Lenny."

"How is it down there?"

"Oh, it's okay." I heard a girl's voice in the background. "Who's that?"

"Jeanie. Jealous?"

"A little."

"We saw Marcus Lipps last night," he said, mentioning the illustrious Spooner alum who was now part of the Andy Warhol crowd in the city. "We did coke until four a.m."

"Do you think you could go check on Katrina today? And call me down here if you find out anything."

"Sure."

"Thanks. See you in about a week."

I hung up, called Manhattan information, and got the number of the Sherry Netherland. An officious male voice answered, "Front desk."

"May I have Jean Clark's suite please, I'm a friend of her daughter's, who I think may be there, in the suite, I mean."

"Miss Clark is not in residence at the moment."

"I know she isn't, she's in Switzerland, I'm looking for her daughter, Katrina, we go to school together. Can you give me the suite's phone number?"

"That's against hotel policy."

I took a deep breath and tried to marshal some charm, "Listen, I'm sure I'm a huge nuisance, I'm very sorry to bother you, but Katrina Felt, Miss Clark's daughter, told me to call her at the hotel." There was a pause and I jumped back in, "*Any* information you can give me would be deeply appreciated."

He tutted, and finally said, "No one has been in Miss Clark's suite for almost a month."

I hung up and sat in the booth with the door closed, anxiety creeping over me like an army of bugs—where, oh where, could my Katrina be? Two dinosaurs trudged through the lobby. I envied them, old and spent, with nothing to worry about but their next cocktail.

HANGING OVER THE whole vacation like a guillotine was Mom's bombshell at the Japanese restaurant. I was certainly curious, but I wasn't about to bring it up myself.

Ann and I had adjoining rooms, and two nights before we flew back I knocked on the door between them. "Ann?"

"Yes, Arthur," she answered in the tone of mild exasperation she usually used with me.

I walked in. Ann was a redhead and had made the mistake of falling asleep in the sun our second day on the island—the result had been a blistering sunburn that was only now beginning to heal. She was sitting up in bed reading some foreign policy tome, wearing a sleeveless nightgown, every inch of exposed skin covered with thick white salve. I sat on the edge of the bed.

"How's the book?"

"Don't patronize me."

"God, Ann."

"This book happens to be fascinating, and important. I don't think it would hurt you one whit to read it. Arthur, I know what goes on at that Spooner School, it has a reputation as one of the biggest druggie schools on the East Coast. I mean, what are you planning on doing with your life, anyway?" she said, putting down the book and eyeballing me intently.

"Do I have to decide right this second?"

"You might want to start thinking about it. Mom and Dad are worried about you."

"Has Mom mentioned something to you about something?"

"That was a very poorly constructed sentence."

"I mean has she said anything about Dad telling us something?" Ann could tell, in that special way siblings can, that I was serious.

"No."

Now I was sure it had to do with my being gay—Dad was going to tell me they suspected I was homosexual and it was okay and they loved me, but they would like me go see some hotshot shrink anyway, just in case. I decided to beat them to the punch, at least with my own sister.

"You know I'm gay, Ann."

She went dead still, staring at me. I felt absolutely vulnerable— she was my big sister. I waited. She seemed to be scrutinizing me to make sure this wasn't another put on. Satisfied, her eyes filled with tears.

"Oh, Arthur, I'm so sorry."

That was about the worst thing she could have said. I remembered a hayride we'd taken up on an apple farm in Vermont when we were little—one of the other kids had made fun of my two-tone

Oxfords and Ann had told him to shut up or she was going to push him off the wagon. I'd loved her so much at that moment.

"Do Mom and Dad know?" she asked. I shook my head, she just kept staring at me—she looked so ridiculous with all that white salve on her face. "Who does know?"

"My friends at school. I have some friends now, a best friend even, who knows I'm gay and doesn't care, in fact she likes it," I said, wishing I were with Katrina.

"I suppose you all take drugs and talk about things like that."

"Ann, I'm gay, that's what I am."

"You're seventeen years old, how do you know what you are?"

"I had sex with a boy at school."

"That's disgusting."

That one hit like a ton of bricks. "Yeah, at least I've had sex."

"Arthur, you're impossible. And you're not a homosexual, you just think it's modern and *hip* and all that shallow nonsense. You're pulling all of this to get attention and it's hopelessly juvenile."

I got up and went to the window: the moon shone on the sea, the air smelled like some tropical flower I couldn't pronounce; my head was reeling, life seemed absurd, I didn't know what I was doing on this faraway island with these people I couldn't talk to. I suddenly had an image of my family as tiny miniature people, screaming up at me, receding and irrelevant.

"I'm sorry I told you," I said, not turning to her.

"If it is true, I don't think you should tell anyone else, it will make your life a lot more difficult."

I turned to her. "I can't believe you'd sit there and tell me that. Do you want me to live a lie? You're supposed to be my sister, Ann—*my sister*."

She couldn't face me—she reached for the tube of salve on her bedside table, squeezed some in her palm, and made a great show of putting a new coat of the greasy white stuff all up and down her arms. She recapped the tube and looked at me. "All right, Arthur. I am your sister. If you're a homosexual I love you and accept you."

When we were little we used to wrestle all the time, and lie touching when we watched TV. We never touched anymore. I wanted to go sit on the bed next to her and touch her, feel her skin, smell her sweet clean smell.

"I want to tell Mom and Dad."

"You *should* tell Mom and Dad."

My stomach flip-flopped—I was hoping she'd tell me *not* to tell Mom and Dad. "You think so?"

"Absolutely. You're right, you shouldn't pretend. There's a small organization of homosexual students at Antioch. I read one of their pamphlets, they believe homosexuals are an oppressed minority just like blacks and American Indians. I'm not sure I subscribe to that theory—homosexuals were not brought to this country as slaves, nor was their land taken from them and their culture destroyed. However, I've read enough anthropology to know that homosexuality exists in all cultures and always has." She folded her hands in her lap. "So you're a homosexual, Arthur?" she said, as if realizing it for the first time.

Suddenly I loved her all over again. I nodded.

"My brother is a homosexual," she announced to herself—I almost expected her to add "Has a ring to it."

"And proud of it," I said, trying to sound convincing.

"And 'gay' is the preferred appellation?"

"Yes."

"So you're *gay*, Arthur." She smiled at me in that self-conscious way people with no sense of humor do. "Well, I certainly hope you'll join a gay rights organization on your campus next year."

I assured her I would, and went downstairs to try reaching Katrina again.

⁓

LUNCH WAS A determinedly festive affair, served under a thatched cabana on the beach. A long buffet table was set out and a tall black man stood beside it playing a steel drum. There was a small bar where a smiling bartender used a blender to whip up all sorts of rum cocktails made with fresh fruit, which the sodden dinosaurs lapped up with smacking lips, walking slowly back for seconds and then thirds and then fourths, many of them ignoring the buffet entirely.

"This is the most alcoholic crowd I have ever seen in my life. And I spent a month in Dublin once," Mom said, in a cheery mood because we were leaving the next morning.

"They do drink, don't they?" Ann said. This was the first time she had ventured outside since her burn and she was covered from head to toe: white cotton gloves, a hat the size of a pizza pie, her face smeared with the gooey white salve, and enormous movie star sunglasses, which she managed to render entirely unglamorous.

I was on my second blender whoopee myself and they were doing their job—my loneliness and anxiety about Katrina were receding, replaced with a rummy benevolence: I decided that I loved this island, I loved my family, I loved the dinosaurs, and most of all I loved the bartender.

Then Mom said, "Charles, I think it's time for you to talk to the children."

An awful dread pushed my booze head to one side of my skull and filled up the empty space with gray fear.

"I'm going to go start packing," Mom said, leaving Dad to twist in the wind solo. I could tell he was relieved she was gone. I wondered if he was going to try and get out of it. Whatever *it* was.

Like the awkward kid called up to the blackboard, Dad squirmed. Ann and I exchanged a glance, but behind the shades and beneath the salve, I couldn't tell what it held. "Ann, Arthur . . ." he began, before stopping to light a cigarette. I was surprised he got that far.

"Come on, Daddy, what's the big hue and cry?" Ann said.

I could see how painful this was for him; he looked like a lost little kid. "Well, you know . . . the apartment in New York, your schools, our vacations . . . vacations like this one." He looked around. "Lots of fuddyduddies," he said, smiling at us. His smile made me sad.

"Is this about money?" Ann said to help him out.

There was a long pause. "Umm . . . well, in a sense. You see, it costs quite a bit, a lot, in fact . . . doctors, dentists—shoes, do you know what shoes cost nowadays?"

"Come on, Daddy, get to the point," Ann said. She took off the sunglasses to show how earnest she was—the only problem was she now looked like Marcel Marceau.

"Well, as you know, I get involved in my projects. Which are important, I think . . ."

"So do I, Daddy," Ann said.

"And fascinating," Daddy said.

"Very fascinating," Ann said.

"However, they often don't generate a great deal of . . . *income.*"

"Which, of course, is the one great sin in America," Ann said.

"Yes, well. I suppose the point is that you both may have to . . . well . . . get jobs next year. I mean, you know, something part time, just to help with . . . so you can, well, pay for some, just some little things, yourself." He let loose a sigh of relief.

After the emotional drum roll I'd been pounding out, this seemed like a puny payoff. And sitting by the Caribbean sipping a blender whoopee, the idea of a job seemed pretty abstract. The fact was I never really thought about money at all, where it came from, any of that stuff. "Nice people don't talk about money," was one of Mom's abiding maxims, and since Dad was an heir I just assumed that we were rich and always would be. I was used to taking the charge cards and heading over to Saks or B. Altman's, to signing for what I wanted at the drugstore and the deli. We were raised to have concern for the less privileged and when I passed tenement windows riding the subway I felt deeply sorry for the occupants, but, on some level, I still thought everyone spent at least a month in Bridgehampton every summer.

"I hope Arthur knows what this means," Ann said.

"I can get a job, Ann. Christ, what do you think I am?"

"I don't think you want me to answer that. I think what Daddy is trying to tell us, and it's something—to tell you the truth, Daddy—that I've suspected for some time, is that the MacDougals have been living well above their means and their means are now running low." She seemed downright happy with the development—I guess it increased her identification with the unwashed masses of the Third World.

Dad nodded.

"Perilously low, Father?" Ann said, practically rubbing her hands together in glee.

"Well, I wouldn't say that," Dad said, although his tone said otherwise.

"I'm going to get another drink. Would anybody like one?" I said.

"Arthur," Ann scolded.

"Not for me, thanks," Dad said.

As I walked over to the bar, the shaded sand felt almost chilly under my feet.

17

THE BUS PULLED over, the driver swung open the door. I stepped out into the night and started up the drive—the ground was covered with snow and the oaks' bare branches scraped in the wind. I'd come back to school a day early to find Katrina.

The boys' dorm was empty. I dropped off my bag and walked up the hill to the darkened split-level, the girls' dorm. The front door opened with a spooky creak, I felt along the wall and switched on the lights. The house was 1950s modern with an open floor plan—the kitchen giving way to the dining area which gave way to the sunken living room, the whole expanse ending in a flagstone fireplace wall. The vast unfurnished space looked like an Edward Hopper painting—lonely, empty, but somehow infused with a human presence.

I walked down the hall to Sapphire and Katrina's room. It was decorated with fringed lampshades, Indian print bedspreads, and chic silk throw pillows that looked like they were in the wrong movie. Both beds were neatly made but there were no signs of recent life. On one of the dressers there was a framed photo of Katrina as a little girl, taken beside a pool, with Jean Clarke on one side of her and Morris Felt on the other. The Bel Air colors were so blazing and everyone was smiling so hard that the image hardly looked real. I opened the top dresser drawer—there was a jumble of underwear with the top of a prescription bottle peeking out. I picked it up: Seconal, from a pharmacy in Beverly Hills, written for Jean Clark. I rummaged around and other bottles appeared: Benzedrine, Valium, Dexedrine, Haldol; some were written for Katrina, others for her mother, from pharmacies in California, New York, Switzerland. I closed the drawer.

I headed back down the hill and walked over to the field. The world was still, the dark buildings hulking and ominous. I lay down in the snow and felt its thin crust crackle—up in the sky there was a mournful crescent moon; stars began to appear and the earth gave way and I was pulled into the night and it was vast and lonely and awesome.

I heard a car coming up the drive and I looked over: a New York City taxi pulled up to the main house, Katrina got out, the cab drove off. She had no luggage, no pocketbook. She stood there for a moment, in her elegant black coat, black slacks, and high heels, then she sat on the front steps, just as she had the day we first met, and lit a cigarette.

I walked over to her; she didn't notice me until I was almost on her. "Hi."

She leaned back on an elbow and looked up at me—she looked world-weary, and it seemed to take her a moment to realize who

I was. Then she tossed aside her cigarette, leaped up, and threw
her arms around my neck, "Oh, Artie, it's *so good* to see you." She
squeezed me tight and then pulled back and looked me in the eyes,
"I missed you fearsome terrible." Then she kissed me lightly on
the lips.

"Where have you been?"

"London."

"Just like that?"

"I'm a jet set kid."

I sat down on the step to get my bearings, and she joined me. "When
did you leave, where did you stay, you don't have any luggage?"

"I got bored here, so I went."

"What did you do over there?"

"I slept with Steve McQueen."

"Really?"

"Well, I *was* a little high, but I'm pretty sure it was Steve
McQueen. Anyway, it was meaningless, but he is awfully cute. How
was the Caribbean?"

"Oh, it was okay, I guess. Family, you know."

"Yeah."

"But, Katrina, I mean what did you do, you just went to the airport one morning and got on a plane?"

"Arthur, they know me at the Dorchester. I have pots of friends
in London, I went to parties, I shopped, I ordered from room service. It was all quite lover-ly, a delicious exercise in acting out. Not
that Mummy will notice, although when the bills come in . . . I was
naughty, I flew first class." She took out her flask and took a deep
swallow. She held it out to me. I shook my head, she shrugged and
took another deep pull.

"Are you all right, Katrina?"

"Dandy."

"Are you sure?"

"Quite sure, old chum. Look, I brought you a present." She reached into her coat and pulled out a small porcelain ashtray with Queen Elizabeth's face on it.

"Thanks. It's great."

"Isn't it nutty, though—an ashtray? So people can put out their cigarettes in the Queen's face."

"It is nutty," I said, looking at the Queen, dowdy and solemn.

"By the way, my lunch with Kander and Ebb went swimmingly, they're darling boys, the musical is almost finished, and they're definitely interested in me."

All these developments left me feeling a little jealous, dizzy, disconnected from Katrina. "That's wonderful," I said.

"I suppose." She hooked her arm in mine. "Now come on, Artie, walk me home."

18

I WAS AWAKENED by the intense smoke from a Gauloise, which always reminded me of French train stations. I looked over to see Nicholas sitting on the edge of his bed, deeply tanned, clean and rested, looking, in spite of himself, the very model of a Jewish-American prince. Except that he was chewing on one corner of his lower lip between puffs. "Good morning, starshine." I gave him a sleepy smile. "Dad's little chippy was named Jacqueline, she was hideously cheerful, changed clothes three times a day, and chattered constantly about movements in art and the history of Far Eastern languages and other topics too headachy to even think about. Dad confided to me that she gave great head—after that I found her amusing. God, it's good to be back." He snuffed out his cigarette and lay back on the bed. "How was wherever the hell you went?"

"It was okay."

"Did they spring the big news on you?"

"Yeah."

"What was it?"

"Oh, just that my dad doesn't have a lot of money left, I guess," I said, feeling a little bit like I was betraying my family.

"Nothing like liberal guilt to eat up a fortune."

"I think it means I have to get a job next year."

Nicholas propped up on an elbow and looked at me. "That *is* a drag."

"Yeah." The whole way I looked at my future had changed—the field of dreams was defaced by a billboard reading GET A JOB.

"Listen, I have an obscene trust fund, plus mother left me every-thing in a subtle little dagger to Dad's heart, I mean safe deposit boxes full of jewelry I've never even looked at. Not to mention the Legers and Mondrians. I'm sure if you're ever really down and out I can loan you twenty bucks."

I gave a mirthless little laugh. But I knew things had changed, we were now on different sides of a very big fence.

Just then a lanky boy, with dirty blond hair and square features, carrying a duffel bag, appeared in the doorway.

"Hi," I said.

"Who are you?" Nicholas asked.

"I'm Phil."

"And you're coming into Spooner *now*?"

Phil looked taken aback. "Yup . . . My family just moved east, from Michigan. It was a last-minute thing, my dad got transferred."

He seemed nice enough. "Well, welcome."

"You're a senior?" Nicholas asked.

Phil nodded. "Um, listen, can I take any room?"

"I guess, wherever you see an empty bed," I said.

"Thanks." He gave us an ingratiating smile. "Say, do you guys know where I can score some pot?"

"No, I really don't," Nicholas said.

"Are you sure, I have money. Here." He reached into his pocket, pulled out a crumpled wad of bills, and offered us a twenty. "Take this and buy me some pot when you can, okay?"

"I don't want your money," Nicholas said with a dismissive laugh.

"Why don't you give him a little of your pot?" I suggested.

Nicholas shot me a look and then sighed. "Okay."

He went to the desk and took out his stash—Phil lit up. Nicholas found an envelope, stuffed some pot in it, and handed it to Phil.

"Puff the magic dragon, lived by the sea," Phil sang, smiling and way off key. "Want to smoke some with me?"

"Not me, thanks," I said.

"Some other time. But, listen, welcome to Spooner," Nicholas said, putting a hand on the door.

"So just take any room that looks empty," I said.

"I'll do that," Phil said. Then he swung his duffel bag over his shoulder and headed down the hall.

THAT NIGHT I went to visit Jeffrey, and found him lying on his bed eating Twizzlers and reading *Maurice*. His room was neat and orderly, with a small teddy bear on top of his dresser. He had filled out since September, and seemed less anxious.

"How's that book?"

"It's so good, Arthur. I find the English upper-class's sexual obsession with the working class so ironic."

"Now that you mention it, so do I. How was your Christmas?"

"It was better than I expected."

"You mean with your folks?"

"Yes." He sat up cross-legged. "I decided I'm not going to take any more of their crap." He smiled at me with matter-of-fact resolve.

"Did you tell them that?"

"No, but I showed them. I don't engage anymore. I'm gay and if they don't like it they can go to hell. I told them I want to go to public school next year. Two years after that I'll be out of the house."

I felt like such a coward, and I was jealous.

"Good for you," I managed. "Listen, Jeffrey, could I ask you a big favor?"

"Sure."

"Do you think you could give me your psychiatrist's name and number?"

"You want to see my psychiatrist?"

"I want to ask him some questions. Do you like him? I mean, is he a nice man?"

"I think he is a nice man, Arthur. Just talking to him has helped me to sort things out in my own mind, if you know what I mean. Is something wrong?"

"Well, not with me, really. I mean, of course with me. But that's not what I want to talk to him about."

Jeffrey smiled at me in a bemused way—I felt as if our roles had been reversed. "Have you told your parents that you're gay, Arthur?"

I picked up the teddy bear and noted that it wasn't a Steiff—so what if I didn't have the courage to come out to my folks, I had the better teddy bear.

"You should," Jeffrey said, leaning forward, his voice growing fervent. "If everyone came out it wouldn't be a big deal anymore. There are *millions* of gay people and we deserve the same rights as everyone else, but they won't give them to us, we have to *demand* them."

"Yeah . . . listen, about your psychiatrist."

19

MISS WATKINS SAT at the upright piano in the assembly hall, playing lightly as students and faculty filed in. There was a just-back-from-vacation feel—lots of tans and new sweaters. When we were all seated, Edward Spooner appeared, walked over to the oak library table, and lifted the rusted old bell—*clang-clang*. Silence spread over the room.

"Good morning and welcome back," he said with a strained smile.

We students were in the middle of the room. Mr. Tupper and his allies were on one side of us, the Scientists and their allies on the other.

"Well, we've left shore and reached the open seas. There's no turning back, our sails are unfurled, picking up faint breezes and mighty gusts alike," Mr. Spooner began, his voice melodious and clipped, almost evangelical. "There have been some pitches and swells, and there are sure to be rough seas ahead. There might even be a hint of mutiny from sailors frightened by the freedom and possibility of our journey." His eyes lighted on Mr. Tupper for a split second. "But glory is not for the faint of heart. Yes, this is indeed a wondrous journey, a voyage of discovery in quest of . . . ?"

Someone ventured, "Happiness?"

Mr. Spooner cocked his head to the side, considering "happiness."

"I can't be happy when black girls are bombed in churches," a Volvo said.

"Ourselves, we're questing for ourselves," someone said.

"Truth."

"Beauty."

"Happiness . . . ourselves . . . truth . . .beauty . . ." Mr. Spooner said, weighing each word.

"Goo-goo!" Katrina called out.

Mr. Spooner's eyebrows went up. "Goo-goo?"

"Yes, darling, *goo-goo*—whatever it is that jazzes you, gets the sparks crackling, makes your shorthairs stand up. Everyone has to find their goo-goo."

"Oh, honestly," Mr. Tupper muttered loudly.

"I rather like that: goo-goo," Mr. Spooner said. "We're on a voyage to discover . . . goo-goo."

Mr. Tupper stood up. "I'd like to say a few words. Last semester, discipline around here was . . ."

Mr. Spooner nodded at Miss Watkins, and she began to play and sing:

"'Tis a gift to be simple
'Tis a gift to be free. . ."
Mr. Spooner, Miss Wimple, and the other Scientists joined in.
"'Tis a gift to come down
Where we ought to be. . ."
Several students took up the singing, including Katrina.

"I'm trying to talk here," Mr. Tupper said, his voice rising, his face flushing.

"And when we find ourselves in the place just right
T'will be in the valley of love and delight."

"And goo-goo!" Katrina added—as Mr. Tupper stormed out of assembly.

20

THERE WASN'T MUCH goo-goo in January. The struggle between the Spooner and Tupper forces seemed to preoccupy the faculty, and the mood on campus kind of curdled. Teachers aligned with Mr. Tupper grew strict and demanding, banned smoking in their classrooms, and handed out copious amounts of homework. In response the Spooner forces grew more lenient and freeform, shunning formal homework and allowing students to run classes. There were clandestine little pow-wows going on in the corners—this one didn't talk to that one—things were definitely building to some sort of shoot-out at the Christian Science corral.

Then there was the matter of the weather. I had never spent a winter in the country and I found it profoundly depressing. Forget the Industrial Revolution, people moved to the cities because they're brighter, cozier, easier, and a lot more fun. Bare trees, packed snow, knife-like winds—being outdoors was hell. And there were no movie theaters, bookstores, or Automats to escape to. Plus it got dark at about three in the afternoon, and the rest of the day and evening stretched in front of you like a black chasm.

It was a bright cold day in the last week of January and we were in Sophia Newcomb's class Discussing *Laugh-In*. There was a knock on the cabin door and then Mr. Tupper poked his head in, looking very serious and self-important. "Could I see Nicholas Meyers and Arthur MacDougal, please?"

The whole class could tell from his tone that something was up; they turned to us with big question marks. Nicholas and I looked at each other, and he shrugged nonchalantly.

We followed Mr. Tupper across the green—his grave look had a self-righteous tinge and I thought I caught a tiny smile flickering at the corners of his mouth.

A police car stood in front of the boys' dorm.

I turned to Nicholas just as he turned to me—he wasn't nonchalant anymore. Time grew slower and slower, the police car larger and larger, the blue sky was frozen in place, the gravel underfoot was throwing tiny fragments of light into my eyes.

"Some gentlemen want to see you," Mr. Tupper said as we headed up the dorm's front steps. The screen door slammed shut behind us, Mr. Tupper walked down the hall, we hung back, he turned and gestured us on with a stern nod.

There were two uniformed policemen in my room—blondish, sturdy, you could see them working at thinking, at putting things together.

I immediately went into crisis/freakout mode, which for me meant freezing stock still, my body temperature plummeting.

"Your name?" the older cop asked me.

It took me a moment to gather my thoughts, which were racing around in mad calamitous circles, and another moment to connect them to my voice.

"My name?" I squeaked.

"Yeah, your name."

"It's, um, Arthur MacDougal."

"Is this your room?"

"Yes."

"You're under arrest."

I felt like I was going to throw up.

Mr. Tupper was standing in the doorway. Phil came up behind him, his face had changed, it was older, smarter. "Phil?" I said, as it clicked that he was a narc. And I'd been nice to him, encouraged Nicholas to *give* him the pot.

Phil looked right through me. They read me my rights. The cold handcuffs closed around my wrists with a metallic snap and the younger cop took my arm and herded me down the hall as doomsday scenarios cascaded through my brain: expulsion, a trial, jail.

"That's not enough pot to get a parakeet stoned, for Christ's sake," I heard Nicholas protesting.

Most of the school was gathered outside, in clusters, watching, worried. Sapphire yelled, "Freedom now!" with righteous rage. Suddenly Katrina rushed up to me, breathless, full of resolve, and grabbed my arm. I had a sudden urge to break away from the cop, run away with Katrina—but where? To the girls dorm and hide under a bed?

"Don't worry, Arthur," she said, "don't worry about a thing."

Her words were a balm, even though it was too late to rewind this nightmare. "Young lady, you'll have to . . ." one of the officers began.

Katrina turned on him, threw back her shoulders, and admonished: "I beg your pardon, good sir, but I am speaking to my friend." The officer stepped back. She leaned into my ear and whispered, "I'll have you sprung in a jiff."

~

THE POLICE STATION was just a few rooms, painted institutional green, in the town hall. The cops were professional, even slightly deferential, as they booked and fingerprinted me. I had settled into a dull shock. "We've got a murder a minute in this country and you're wasting money on shit like this? Unbelievable!" I heard Nicholas rant from the next room.

Mom answered the phone. "Yes?"

"Hi, Mom, it's Arthur," I said, trying to sound casual.

"What's wrong?"

I was sitting in a small conference room, a cop watching me through the open door.

"I've been arrested."

"You've *what?*"

"Been arrested."

"What for?"

"Marijuana." There was a pause the Macy's parade could have marched through. "Mom . . . ?"

"Well, Arthur, I really don't know what to say." Her voice was taut with barely controlled anger. "Where are you?"

"At the police station."

I heard her light a cigarette. "Your father is at the Bronx Zoo, he's developed a sudden obsession with six-toed sloths . . . Jesus Christ, how could you have let this happen?"

"I'm sorry."

"As well you might be . . . Let me make some calls. What's your number there? I'll call you back."

As I hung up, Nicholas was led in, smiling—he was taking this better than I was, or at least pretending to.

"What did your father say?"

"He said I was a worthless piece of shit. You have to understand, the term's an endearment to my old man. Did you see the amount of pot they're charging us with?"

"The whole thing is kind of a drag though, isn't it?"

"A minor inconvenience. Boy, that Tupper is a real Benedict Arnold."

"He was behind it, huh?"

"Oh yeah. Did you see the look on his face? He was practically licking his chops."

"Why'd he do it?"

"Power, baby, with a healthy dose of class rage tossed in the mix. He's a bumpkin with a chip on his shoulder the size of Elsie the cow. He thinks everyone at Spooner looks down at him. Which is true. This was his way of getting attention. It's basically a tantrum. I hope Edward ships him back to moo-moo land triple time."

Hearing Nicholas rant, I actually started to feel protective of Mr. Tupper—he was a fish out of water at Spooner, he never should have been there, but . . . he *was* there.

An older cop came into the room.

"Arthur MacDougal, you're free to go."

I walked down the hall half-expecting them to tell me they were kidding. But there was Katrina, standing by the front counter beside an enormous basket of fruit, cheese, and candy; several officers were clustered around her. "Then Bing stood on the diving board, sang a chorus of *High Hopes*, and did the *worst* belly flop you've *ever* seen in your life!"

The officers laughed adoringly. Katrina turned and gave me a tiny wink. She looked highly respectable in a just-bought wool coat, tailored navy mid-calf dress with large white buttons up the front, and sensible black flats.

"Arthur, darling, I was hoping they'd keep you just a bit longer, I'm having so much fun with my new friends." The officers beamed. "But I suppose we must run along. Thank you so much for taking such good care of my friend, I know we'll have this whole little misunderstanding straightened out in no time."

"But, Katrina, did you pay my bail?"

Katrina treated the officers to a gentle roll of her eyes, "Now, now, Arthur, curiosity killed the cat." She slipped her arm through mine and led me outside.

There was a cab waiting.

I was afraid to give in to my elation, I mean were her machinations even legal? She couldn't have gotten me out on charm alone, could she?

"How did you do this?" I asked.

She gave me a wry, triumphant smile. "Movie star magic, darling," she said, slipping into the cab.

21

FOR THE NEXT few weeks, school felt like a ship trying to right itself after being broadsided by a sudden squall. Mr. Spooner was visible around campus, members of the board of trustees were seen coming and going, all radiated chipper resolve; in spite of their best efforts, a half-dozen students were withdrawn by their parents. It turned out Jean Clarke's business manager had paid my bail, which Dad repaid. Nicholas was sprung by his father later that day. Dad also hired a fancy Hartford lawyer, who had called to tell me I would be pleading no contest to the marijuana charge, and that if I weren't arrested again for two years my record would be sealed, there wouldn't be anything that could mar my future job prospects. Yippee.

One evening in mid-February I found Katrina in the library, a pile of papers in front of her, wearing no makeup and simple black glasses, bundled up in a wool sweater and scarf, a beret on her head. To save money, the heat had been turned down in all the buildings and we shivered through the day.

"What are you doing?" I asked.

"Applying to colleges."

"Really?" I asked, sitting down opposite her. Then I remembered that every college I knew of had a deadline long past.

"Believe it or not, yes. You see, Artie, the bust made me realize how much I love this crazy school. I adored *Jane Eyre*, and now I'm reading *Sister Carrie* and loving that. I've never read before, ever. I get a cozy feeling when I'm reading, like I'm in an English manor house on a rainy Sunday." She looked at me for a moment, and then looked down, almost blushing. "And college was your idea to begin with."

She seemed self-possessed, and the glasses gave her a studious look, but was this just another role she was trying on for size?

"So where are you applying?"

"Well, I hate to admit it, but I called my father. He's thrilled, was actually nice to me. He lectures at UCLA sometimes and told me he could get me in there. He also said he has connections at NYU. Isn't it awful using him to get into college?"

"Well, that's the way the world works."

She wrote something on one of the forms and as she was writing she said, "By the way, I heard from my agent, the musical is going to be auditioning in the early spring."

"That's exciting news."

"I guess." She pushed the glasses up on her nose and looked at me. "To tell you the truth, it's part of what goaded me into this. I don't know if I'm ready to join the circus, or if the circus will even want me." She looked scared for a moment, then she raked her fingers through her hair and shook her head. "I wish we could go to college somewhere together."

"Well, I'd never get into UCLA or NYU, but I have applied to L.A. State College, so we'd be in the same city."

She cocked an elbow on the table and rested her cheek on her fist. "Oh, wouldn't that be peachy? We could study together at night, and I could show you *my* L.A., it's full of nooks and crannies, canyons and enclaves, it's a divine mysterious town in its own tacky way."

I felt a sudden surge of affection for her so strong that I thought I might cry. "I'd love that."

We sat quietly for a few moments, listening to the building creaking in the cold.

"It's going to be okay, don't you think?" Katrina asked by and by.

"What?"

"Oh . . . everything."

I wasn't sure *anything* would be okay, in fact I felt like I was tiptoeing on quicksand. Every time I thought I understood Katrina she would do something that surprised or alarmed me, and my own future—college, career (whatever that was), love, sex—seemed unsettled, scary, beyond comprehension. But however tenuous I was, Katrina felt as fragile as an ancient vase, so I answered her with a "Yes."

Then, from upstairs, we heard the sounds of a hymn being played by Miss McCoy, just as we had that first day, back in September, so long ago.

22

IT WAS THE tail end of February. School had settled into an uneasy peace, the two camps communicating with little more than tight smiles. It was strange to go from a classroom where discipline was rigid and homework fixed, to one where you could smoke, call the teacher by his first name, and design your own assignments. Mr. Tupper has succeeded in dampening drug use somewhat, and also in creating a sense of mistrust and unease, as if something terrible could happen at any minute. There was a rumor that Mr. Spooner was out looking for a replacement for Mr. Tupper, and that as soon as he found one he would fire him. We were hoping this would happen, but as Nicholas pointed out, new teachers cost money and that was in short supply.

Katrina, Sapphire, and I were eating lunch. The temperature outside was in the teens, and everyone had scarves wrapped around their necks and two sweaters on. Sapphire was telling us about her plans to spend next year backpacking around Asia and North Africa, when Mr. Tupper strode into the dining room wearing an expression I hadn't seen since the headmaster at Collegiate announced the Kennedy assassination. He went over to the faculty table, leaned down, and whispered something—everyone froze. Then the teachers stood up as one and followed him out.

Within moments angry voices echoed in from assembly hall, there were hurried footfalls on the steps, doors opening and closing. Mr. Tupper reappeared in the doorway. "Classes are cancelled for the rest of the day. Day students will please go home. Boarding students, this building is off limits."

And then he disappeared.

We looked at each other in a mixture of shock and burning curiosity. Sapphire grabbed our hands, "Come on, let's investigate."

We reached the hallway just in time to see Edward Spooner dart down the stairs and into assembly hall. He saw us but didn't look at us.

"What the hell is going on here?" Mr. Tupper's voice boomed from behind the closed doors.

"Can we please calm down?" Mr. Spooner pleaded.

We looked up and saw Miss Wimple standing at the top of the stairs, looking like she'd just seen Mary Baker Eddy going down on the devil.

"What happened?" I mouthed to her.

"Oh children, children . . ."

"Tell us," Sapphire urged.

She put a hand on the banister to steady herself, and whispered, "The faculty's checks . . . *insufficient funds.*"

"What does it mean?" Katrina asked, squeezing my hand.

"I don't know."

"Let's go tell Nicky," Sapphire said.

Nicholas had been subdued since the bust, had taken to staying in bed all day reading comic books. He wouldn't talk about it, but I sensed that things had gotten really ugly between him and his father. We found him engrossed in Spider-Man and told him the news.

"Time to pack our bags," he said.

"Don't say that!" Katrina cried.

"The Christian Science dough dried up. Those folks don't even use drugs for *disease*, for Christ's sake, they're not about to subsidize recreational use." Out the window I could see students milling around in little knots, huddled against the cold, at a loss. "So, either the school is going to close this weekend, or the trustees are going to put the Tuppers in charge of the asylum," he said, reaching for a Gauloise, cheering up for the first time in weeks.

I felt responsible for this latest disaster: why the hell had I told Nicholas to give that narc some of his pot, that's what set the whole spiral in motion, if I had just kept my stupid goody-two-shoes mouth shut. And I'd always thought of schools as solid things—after all, Collegiate had been around for over a century. Was there *anything* in life you could count on?

Katrina sat on the edge of my bed, her lips parted, her eyes filled with uncertainty. I realized that if Spooner folded, she had nowhere else to go.

~

I WAS ONE of only three students at breakfast the next morning, trying to enjoy my corn flakes, not exactly comfort food, especially in a barely heated building. But the cook's check had bounced too, and he was nowhere to be seen.

Suddenly Katrina blew in wearing a short mink coat, mini-skirt, enormous sunglasses, and black high heels. "Artie, come on, I've got a car waiting!"

"Where are we going?"

She grabbed my hand and pulled me up. "You'll see."

We dashed out of the building and hopped into the cab. Katrina snuggled into the corner.

"Where did you get that coat?" I asked.

"It was a hand-me-down from Mom."

The cab was heading toward town. It was a bright frigid day— sunny, sharp, glittery.

"I think Spooner is falling apart, Katrina."

She was quiet for a moment and looked very serious behind the sunglasses. Then she looked out the window and said breezily: "Oh well, darling, things *do* fall apart. The trick is not to fall with them."

We pulled into a parking lot in front of a small one-story white house. A sign outside read: Animal Rescue Society.

"We won't be long, driver," Katrina said, hopping out.

I followed her into the building and was immediately hit by the smells: fur and poop and dog food overlaid with a Lysol tang; and the noise—our entrance set off a round of wild barking. There was a slow-moving old man behind a desk.

"Good morning," he said with a kind smile.

"Good morning, sir, I want to get a kitten," Katrina said.

"Well, I think we have a few of those. If you just go straight back through those doors you'll find all the animals available for adoption. There is a five-dollar fee."

Katrina opened her purse and pulled out a fifty, "Here, take this. A contribution for your good work. But before we look, I should dash to the little girls' room."

"It's right down the hall."

"Back in a sec."

As she turned into the bathroom I caught a flash of her silver flask as she pulled it out of her pocket.

The animals were in two rows of stacked cages and we moved down the line: the cats were pretty cool customers, curled on their blankies, skeptical and haughty; the dogs were plaintive—yapping, jumping, begging for attention, so needy that I couldn't stand to look at them.

"Oh, Artie, look!"

Katrina was down at the last cage. It held one tiny orange-and-white kitten, busy rolling around with a small furry toy. It noticed us, stopped suddenly, on its back, limbs around the toy, and looked at us with bright curious green eyes.

"That is the cutest thing I've ever seen in my life," I said.

With sharp jerky movements the kitty leaped away from the toy and approached the bars of the cage, poked its nose through. Katrina leaned in and bumped noses with it, and the kitten flew back in delighted shock. Katrina opened the cage and lifted out the kitten, snuggled it in the crook of her neck. "Oh, I'm in love."

I wanted to ask if it made sense for her to be getting an animal now, but she looked so happy, rapturous even, that I didn't.

Katrina tipped the kitten over and examined its tummy. "It's a girl. I'll call her Charlotte, after Charlotte Brontë. I know what you're thinking, Artie, and you're wrong, I had animals galore when I was little, and it may surprise you to know that I'm a wonderful mother." She looked down at the kitten in her arms and that Katrina sadness passed over her face.

Then she shook her head, lifted the kitten high up, and bumped noses with it again. "Oh, my darling little Charlotte, my baby girl."

23

ONE AFTERNOON ABOUT a week later, I was lying in bed reading Hedy Lamar's autobiography, *Ecstasy and Me*. Poor Hedy had recently been arrested for shoplifting, and her rags-to-riches-to-rags story was a lesson in how brutally fickle Hollywood could be. Having been arrested myself, I felt I could relate to Hedy in a special way. But while her arrest had been a publicity bonanza, mine had only increased my guilt about what a letdown I was to my folks and how much damage I had done to the school. Nicholas was over on his bed reading *Howl*. I looked out my window and saw a Jaguar pull up to the big house. A middle-aged man, one of the school's trustees, got out and opened the trunk. He stood waiting for a moment, watching the front door. It opened and Mr. Spooner stepped out, head up, hands in his topcoat, radiating a wounded dignity. Miss

Wimple followed him, lugging two suitcases. Mr. Spooner watched as the suitcases were loaded into the trunk. The trustee got in the driver's seat. Edward looked slowly around the campus. Miss Wimple watched him, her mouth quivering.

"Nicholas, look."

He came over. "Poor Spooner."

"Should we go say good-bye?"

"No, that would only add to his humiliation."

They got in the Jaguar and drove off.

The coup had succeeded: within an hour the Tuppers had moved down to the main house, and the next morning Mr. Tupper called an assembly and announced that the Board of Trustees had appointed him interim headmaster, and that there were all sorts of new rules: two hours of quiet in the dorms every night, lights out at eleven, mandatory class attendance, no smoking anywhere, of cigarettes or anything else.

Everyone followed the rules for a day or two and then slacked off; the campus felt lifeless, deflated, a sensation helped along by the dismal late-winter weather. I was waiting to hear from colleges and trying to keep a low profile, unable to shake my gnawing remorse that I was responsible for the school's demise. Katrina's Broadway audition had been scheduled for the first week of April, and her moods swung from excited to anxious to elated to ambivalent.

LENNY AGREED TO give me a ride to Jeffrey's shrink's office, which was in New Haven. It was one of those dank March days with a low gray sky and a wind that cuts through you. We were both pretty quiet on the ride, we listened to rock music on the radio, Lenny sang along on some of the songs. He was being his friendly self but once again had pulled back, he and Jeanie were an official item at this point and I knew that the whole thing between us, whatever it was, was probably hopeless. Still, I couldn't stop myself from being flooded with desire every time I saw that snaggle tooth.

I'd never been to New Haven before and was surprised how run-down, grungy, and gothic it was. The weather didn't help. Lenny dropped me off at Dr. Silberman's office, which was in a red brick row house near the Yale campus. A little buzzer sounded when I walked into the empty waiting room. I sat down on a Swedish modern couch, picked up a copy of *Smithsonian*, and tried to read a story on Zuni pottery, but I was too keyed-up to concentrate. From behind a closed door I could hear low voices.

After about five minutes the door opened and a nervous young man who looked like a Yale student—tall, tousled blondish hair, in tie and blazer—came out and quickly crossed the waiting room without looking at me. After a few moments a middle-aged man, slightly paunchy and sort of homely—big lips and nose, not much chin—came out.

"Arthur MacDougal?" He had a soft calm voice that immediately relaxed me, at least a little.

"Yes."

"Lester Silberman," he said, holding out his hand.

"How do you do?" He had a dead-fish handshake.

"Come on in."

His office was small, lined with bookcases, with a window that looked out on the gray day, a thick Oriental rug, a poster of a Matisse cut-out, a couple of massive maroon leather armchairs. The room felt hushed and safe.

Dr. Silberman indicated one of the chairs and I sat; he sat in the other and picked up a yellow legal pad.

"So, Arthur, you're a friend of Jeffrey Wilcox."

"Yes, I am, doctor, I like Jeffrey."

"And what can I do for you?"

I leaned forward, feeling an urgent sense of purpose, "I have this other friend at school who I'm really worried about."

He raised his eyebrows.

"No, really, I'm not talking about myself and pretending it's someone else, it *is* someone else." No response, he just sat there looking at me, as inscrutable as Buddha. "She's a girl and she's very talented but she drinks quite a bit and I found a lot of pill bottles in her drawer and she's happy one minute and too happy the next and then sad and I just think she's very lonely and hurt and . . . and . . . I don't know. It's sort of scaring me. And I think it's scaring her too. I don't know what else to say, I'm just very, *very* worried about her."

Dr. Silberman was still staring at me in that penetrating way that made me feel exposed and idiotic. After what seemed like an hour he spoke. "Well, Arthur, there really isn't anything I can do for your friend. Without speaking to her myself it's impossible for me to evaluate her. You, on the other hand, seem very anxious."

"Of course I'm anxious, my best friend is in trouble. You don't understand—I love Katrina."

"Tell me a little bit more about how *you're* feeling."

"I'm feeling like screaming. What do you think is happening to Katrina?"

"I really can't comment on that without meeting her."

"Can't you at least help me out a little bit?"

"The symptoms you described could be manifestations of any

number of conditions. Certainly alcoholism or cross-addiction come to mind. But I really think, Arthur, that you should concentrate on yourself."

"I *am* concentrating on myself. I mean I'm concentrating on Katrina, myself is. I feel like she's in some kind of serious trouble and I have to help her."

"Arthur, I think you're getting yourself too worked up."

I felt like I was talking to an overeducated, self-satisfied brick wall. "*You're* getting me worked up. *What should I do to help Katrina?*"

Dr. Silberman set the legal pad down on a small table and folded his hands in his lap. And just sat there.

My head felt like it was about to explode.

"You know what I think, Arthur," he said finally.

"No, what?" I spit out.

"I think the real reason you're here is to discuss your homosexual impulses."

A glint of excitement lit his eyes and I suddenly wondered if it was *his* homosexual impulses that were driving this show.

"That's totally ridiculous. That's a whole other issue and when I want to discuss it with someone I'll tell them. Now, please, can you help me out at all here with Katrina?"

"Arthur, you're getting ahead of yourself. First of all, therapy is never a one-shot process. If you want to begin seeing me you'll have to call your parents and tell them. Then I'll have to discuss the financial arrangements with them. I think, if I may say so, that Jeffrey is making great progress. I would expect that you and I could have a similarly productive relationship."

He looked like a smug little potentate, my frustration was making my muscles twitch.

"I think you're an asshole," I blurted out. I'd never called anyone an asshole in my life before and my first thought was how impolite I'd been. "Listen, I'm sorry, thank you for seeing me, but I'm going to go now."

A cruddy wet snow had started to fall, I looked down the street and saw a sign for the Taft Hotel and headed toward it; I had about a half hour before Lenny would be picking me up.

The Taft lobby was done up mostly in soft browns, with lived-in couches and armchairs. I made a beeline for a bank of phone booths, sat down on the little wooden seat, pushed the folding door closed, and dialed quickly, before my courage cooled.

"Hello?"

"Hi, Mom."

"Arthur. How are you, darling?"

"I'm okay, I guess. Listen, there's something I want to tell you. Is Dad around?"

"Yes."

"Could you ask him to pick up?"

"Are you all right?"

"Yes, Mom. Please get Dad."

I heard her put down the receiver. I pressed a palm against the cool glass of the booth's door.

"Hi, Arthur," Dad said warily.

"I'm on, too," Mom said.

I sat up, took a deep breath, thought of Jeffrey, and leaped. "I wanted to tell you both that I'm gay."

There was a *looooong* pause. Finally I couldn't take it.

"Well, aren't you going to say anything?"

"By gay I assume you mean . . ." Mom began, unable to choke out the word.

"I mean homosexual, yes."

The next pause was only marginally shorter. I could hear their breathing.

"Would you like to see a psychiatrist?" Mom asked hopefully.

I laughed.

"I don't find this conversation the least bit amusing," she said.

"No, I *don't* want to see a psychiatrist. I just wanted to tell you. I already told Ann. Now you all know."

"I don't know what to say," Mom said, and I could hear her crying.

"Esme, we'll discuss this. Son?" He never called me son.

"Yes, Dad."

"I think your mother and I need a little time with this. But thank you for telling us," Dad said, a mix of resignation and kindness in his voice.

I felt the tears welling up behind my eyes and willed them back down; a beautiful young woman crossed the lobby—long-limbed, creamy, wearing a camel cashmere coat, looking like she'd stepped out of a Fitzgerald novel.

"Thanks for saying that, Dad. I'm going to go now."

***

"YOU DON'T LOOK so hot," Lenny said as we headed out of town.

"It didn't go well with the shrink."

Lenny put his hand on the back of my neck and gave me an affectionate squeeze. "Poor kid."

"Could we listen to some classical music?"

"Sure, man."

Lenny found the classical station, they were playing Beethoven, the Mercedes' leather seats were butter soft, the car was deliciously overheated, Lenny was in charge, driving us through the wet snow, it was all soothing. I didn't want to talk and Lenny could sense it, every now and then he'd look over at me; there was so much sympathy in his eyes.

By and by he said: "Listen, there's a small state park with a lake a little ways up ahead. It'll be deserted at this time of year. You want to go park there for a while?"

I hesitated and he reached over and ruffled my hair, letting his hand trail down the back of my neck.

"After all, we do have some unfinished business." He rubbed my neck with his thumb. I moaned involuntarily. "I don't know what the shrink said, but Dr. Solberg thinks you need a little loving."

Then he flicked on his blinker and turned in to the park.

24

LENNY ASKED ME not to tell anyone about our tryst. For the first few days, it was hard not to tell Katrina, but then I found that I loved keeping it our secret. I loved the way it felt when Lenny and I looked at each other across a classroom, co-conspirators, comrades, bound by the flesh in some way that felt real and raw and, for me at least, completely new. One night after dinner Lenny showed up at the dorm and I could tell he wanted a repeat, but there were just too many people around. We did sit side by side on my bed, our shoulders touching, and my whole consciousness focused there, on that place where our bodies touched, and it filled me with warmth and excitement and promise. Suddenly school had a new dimension, which made its otherwise precarious state easier to deal with. I carried my secret, and it carried me.

It was almost April, but nobody told Old Man Winter, and both faculty and students moved from class to class pallid and puffy, dispirited,
lethargic even in the cold. One weeknight, way past midnight, Katrina,
Sapphire, Nicholas, and I were sitting in the darkened dining room,
wide awake with nowhere to go. The old building was still. Outside a
light snow was falling. A candle burned in the middle of the table, high-
lighting the chips, scratches, and primitive initial carvings. We were all
leaning in toward the candle and talking in near whispers.

"April, May, and then it's over," I said, feeling nostalgic already.

"Out into the world," Katrina said in a tiny voice.

"We're almost not children anymore," Sapphire said.

Nicholas ran his fingertip through the flame, "Thank God for that."

Nobody said anything for a long time.

"Are you okay, Nicholas?" Sapphire asked.

"Me? Oh, yeah," he said, trying to sound offhand.

"This school has been your home for four years, Nicky, you've
been happy here."

"Delirious," Nicholas said. "Now drop it."

Sapphire's face grew sad. I ran my fingertip along the grooves of
an *O* carved on the tabletop.

"Come on," Katrina said.

We followed her into assembly hall. We sat on the floor opposite
the bank of windows and watched the snow fall—it was steady now,
fat flakes, calm, white, quiet. Katrina began to hum, low and soft
and soulful, in perfect harmony with the snow. She rested her head
on my shoulder.

The front door opened with a slow creak, as if someone didn't
want to be heard. Edward Spooner walked silently into the room.
He didn't see us. He walked over to the windows and looked out at
the lake and the falling snow.

We watched him watching. Then Sapphire whispered, "Hi."

Mr. Spooner turned and looked at us, half his face in shadow, half lit by the snowy night.

"We miss you," Katrina said.

A sad little smile played at the corners of his mouth.

"I wanted to take a last look," he said, turning back to the window.

"Where are you going, Mr. Spooner?" Sapphire asked.

He crossed to us and knelt with his peculiar grace.

"The actual *where* isn't so terribly important, is it? What about you four, are you making out all right?"

Sapphire's mouth quivered, her eyes shone.

"Dear, sweet Sapphire," Mr. Spooner said.

"This was a wonderful school," she said.

Nicholas looked down and nodded his head, his Adam's apple bobbed. Mr. Spooner put a hand on his knee. "Hold on to what you found here, Nicholas. It's what your mother would want."

Nicholas exhaled sharply and leaned his head back against the wall, his eyes squeezed shut. Sapphire took his hand in both of hers and pressed it to her cheek.

Mr. Spooner turned to Katrina and me. "I'm sorry we had so little time together."

"So am I," Katrina said. Then she looked down. He took her chin in his hand and raised her head. "You're a very gifted young woman, Katrina. We all need help sometimes . . . Will you remember that?"

Katrina nodded. He turned to me.

"I'm waiting to hear from colleges," I said in a preemptive strike.

He gave me a gentle smile. " 'We're not here to dream and drift, we have heavy loads to lift.' "

My old friend guilt gave me a little wave.

Suddenly he sprang up and looked around the room. "I had a vision. A vision of children, bright and eager, minds agile, leaping, grasping . . ." Just as suddenly he deflated, the life went out of his face. He walked to the window. "I am midstream in my journey. I have visited with despair. But I have never surrendered . . ."

The snow was falling quickly now, whiting out the world.

" 'I walk with love along the way / And oh it is a holy day . . .' "

He repeated this again. And then again. He forgot us. As quietly as we could, we got up and left him.

25

I WAS GETTING dressed when I heard a car horn honk outside the boys' dorm—Katrina had hired a limousine to take us into Manhattan for her audition. I grabbed my coat and dashed outside. It was the second week of April and there was a high white sky and a breeze that carried a hint of warmth.

Katrina sat in the far corner of the back seat, her legs tucked under her, looking rested and enchanting in a pair of black cords, white oxford shirt, black cotton v-neck sweater, and tennis sneakers; she smelled fresh and bracing, and once again I marveled at how she was able to pull herself together: she seemed to have an endless supply of fresh starts and new tomorrows.

"One mustn't dress up for auditions, it's all about the work," she announced. "I can't decide if I should sing George Gershwin or Elvis Presley."

"I'd go with the former. Do you know much about the show, or the part?"

"Well, you know, it's Kander and Ebb, Hal Prince is directing, it's set in the fifties, about the daughter of an uptight suburban family who gets involved in the civil rights movement. There's an inter-racial romance. My agent says it's full of heart and pizzazz and has more buzz than ten beehives."

"How's Charlotte?" I asked.

"Divine. She's ferociously bright. Loves to jump on top of my dresser and fling things around the room. She's been awfully good for me. She sleeps on my pillow."

"Do she and Sapphire get along?"

"I think they're both a little jealous of each other. Last night she leaped onto Sapphire's head, claws and all. Did *not* want to let go."

As we sped down the West Side Highway a light rain started to fall, a gentle spring rain. We got off the highway and headed east into Manhattan's grid.

"We'll get out here," Katrina said to the driver.

We were on Ninth Avenue in the Forties. The driver pulled over and we got out and stood on the corner in the rain, surrounded by brick tenements, garages and gas stations, the pink neon of pizza parlors and hair salons. "Isn't this neighborhood a kick?"

"What time is your audition?"

"Eleven-thirty."

"That's in half an hour."

"Don't worry, silly boy, it's just a few blocks from here," Katrina said, grabbing my hand and leading me into a bar.

The Blarney Stone was long and narrow and dim and smelled like damp bar towels and spilled whiskey and tobacco. The bartender had a long face and a large belly, about a half a dozen decrepit men sat along the bar. Katrina waltzed up and perched on a stool, I sat beside her. The men glanced at us with mild interest and then went back to their solitary drinking.

"I'd like a Johnny Walker straight up, with a beer chaser," Katrina said to the bartender.

"You old enough to drink?"

"Yes, sir, have been for years," Katrina said with tongue-in-cheek solemnity.

The bartender considered for a moment and then looked at me.

"Just a ginger ale, please."

He went off to get our drinks.

"Katrina, should you be drinking right before your audition?"

"Isn't this place divinely cozy?"

"Katrina . . ."

She took out her Dunhills and lit one. Our drinks arrived and she took a small sip of her scotch and purred with pleasure. "What could be more romantic than sitting in a divey bar at eleven in the morning on a rainy Manhattan day?"

"I can think of a lot of things."

"Oh, Artie, don't be a pill." She slid off her stool, scotch in hand, and went over to the jukebox, which she perused with exaggerated interest—she looked like she was in one of those fashion spreads where chic models are juxtaposed against seedy locations. I sipped my ginger ale, which was way too syrupy-sweet. Katrina punched in her selections, polished off her drink, came back to the bar, and downed her glass of beer in one swallow. "Another, please," she called to the bartender as Aretha Franklin began to sing about the first snow in Kokomo.

I was growing more anxious by the second. Was I a terrible friend? Was I an uptight asshole? Was I both? I pointed to the clock above the bar, which read eleven-fifteen. "Katrina, look at the time."

"Don't you know by now, darling, that I thrive on the edge, it's where I want to be, where I feel most alive."

"But this could be important for your career, your life."

"I know what I'm doing, dear boy, I can feel my juices rising right now and they're going to peak—*pow!*—when I hit that stage. You watch me, kiddo."

Her second round arrived. It may have been scotch but it looked like disaster to me.

"Katrina, *please* don't drink it."

She looked at me long and hard. "You really are a true friend, aren't you, Artie? Do you know how much I love you?" Then she put down the drink, threw some bills on the bar, grabbed my hand, and we were off.

The rain was coming down steadily now and I felt a kick of adrenaline as Katrina led me on a giddy dash east. We arrived at the Ethel Barrymore Theater at exactly eleven-thirty.

There was a middle-aged woman in the lobby, wearing half glasses, holding a clipboard, waiting. Katrina's eyes were flashing and her smile was a little lopsided.

"Hi, I'm Katrina Felt."

"Of course. Just a moment," the woman said deferentially, before pushing through the swinging doors and into the theater.

Katrina gulped air, she was keyed to an elated pitch. "Are you going to be all right?" I asked, and was answered with a Kewpie doll face, all wide eyes and pursed lips. I was torn between concern and excitement.

The woman reappeared. "They'll see you now."

"My friend is going to watch from the back of the house," Katrina said, pulling me through the swinging doors.

I took a seat in one of the last rows. The theater was huge and ornate, filled with plush reds and golds, there were about a dozen grown-ups spread across two rows down front. Katrina skipped—*skipped!*—down the center aisle and up a short flight of steps onto the stage. She shaded her eyes and looked out.

"Hello, I'm Katrina Felt," she said with a big smile. There was a chorus of "hellos" in response. Was I the only one who could tell she'd been drinking?

And then she began to sing:

> *There's a somebody I'm longing to see*
> *I hope that he*
> *Turns out to be*
> *Someone who'll watch over me*

Her voice filled the empty theater effortlessly—sound that poured over me, liquid and luscious—the cavernous space seemed to disappear, there was nothing but Katrina's voice and presence, vulnerable, captivating, heart-rending. The people up front leaned forward, exchanged looks.

Then she stopped midnote and said, "Oh shit, I fucked up."

My stomach clenched—*I* fucked up, letting her have that drink.

Katrina stood with hands on hips, head cocked, lower lip out. There was nervous laughter from the grown-ups.

"Wrong note. May I start from the top?"

"Please," a man called out.

I'm a little lamb who's lost in the wood
I know I could
Always be good
To one who'll watch over me.

This time she sailed through it and a palpable excitement coursed through her audience, which broke into applause. Katrina smiled and took a little bow. "Thank you *so much*," she said, as if they'd given her something priceless.

⁓

"**Do you think** they liked me?" Katrina asked as the limousine headed uptown through the rain.

"*Liked* you? They *adored* you. You were fantastic, I was so proud of you."

"Oh, Arthur, thank you. Hal Prince gave me a big smile."

I had no doubt they were going to offer her the part. Part of me was thrilled but I was also sad—Katrina was going to have a big-time life and I doubted there would be much room in it for her nerdy little high-school best-friend-*du-jour*. In six weeks Spooner would be over and she would be off on her rocket ship, while I sputtered along in my Rambler, heading . . . who knows where? She had chosen me to be her friend because I was easy, needy, and available. I was eminently replaceable.

"Why the long face, darling?"

"Nothing."

"Oh, Artie, you're a little bit jealous, aren't you?"

"No!" I scoffed. Then I had an idea. "Listen, do you mind if we detour over to Broadway and Sixty-seventh?"

"Of course not."

I walked into the lobby of the Regency Theater, the city's best revival house and one of my favorite haunts. I'd never applied for a job before and my heart was thump-thumping in my chest.

"I'd like to speak to the manager, please, if possible," I said to the man tearing tickets for the early afternoon show. He pointed me across the lobby to a door marked OFFICE. I knocked.

"Come in."

The small room was cluttered with film cans, and smelled like old cigar smoke and cold coffee, there was a desk chaotic with papers, a *Rear Window* poster on the wall above it. I recognized the manager, a burly middle-aged man with a tired face.

"Hello, my name is Arthur MacDougal."

He smiled at me in a distracted way. "And what can I do for you, Arthur MacDougal?"

"I love your theater, I come quite a lot, I live just down on Central Park South."

"Glad you like us," he said, studying a light-blue form.

"I am, ah, looking for a summer job, I know it's still a few months away, but I thought it's never too early, you know."

The manager turned his attention to me, looking me up and down and then in the eye. "So you like old movies?"

"I love them."

"Well, why don't you give me your name and number and I'll put you at the top of my list. I usually do need extra help during the summers, the heat drives up our business."

"Thank you, sir."

I was exultant as I climbed back in the car. I'd actually done something about my future, and suddenly I felt less helpless, almost a little like a grown-up, maybe.

"I need a drink," Katrina said. "Let's pay Mummy a pop visit."

A visit with Jean Clarke! This was turning into my day of days.

⁓

THE ENTRYWAY OF Jean Clarke's apartment at the Sherry-Netherland had walls upholstered in pale pink brocade that made it look like the inside of a jewelry box; through an archway, the living room glittered and glowed.

"Mom, I'm home," Katrina called out, and shot me an ironic glance.

Then Jean Clarke appeared. She looked . . . well, small—she was a tiny thing, almost like a normal person who had been shrunk down one size by a science-fiction machine. But once I got past that, I took in auburn hair, shoulder length and flipped under, that shone like a newly waxed car, and that famous pixie face that could play everything from English aristocrat to Great Depression migrant. She had on serious makeup and was wearing a flaring navy-blue mid-thigh dress covered with big white polka dots. When she saw Katrina she broke into an enormous smile.

"Darling!" She went to her daughter and gave her a pursed peck on the lips.

"Hi, Mom," Katrina said, beaming.

Then Jean Clarke turned to me and said a warm "Hello."

"Arthur MacDougal, it's a pleasure to meet you."

"Oh, what lovely manners. Katrina, you look adorable."

"You look great, too, Mom."

"Oh, stop it. But do you like this dress?" She twirled like a girl primping for the prom—that Jean Clarke energy and charm! "It's Mary Quant. Your mom's gone Mod."

"What the hell's going on out there?" a husky woman's voice called from the living room.

Jean Clarke grabbed both our hands and led us in—one entire wall of the vast room was covered with a smoky mirror veined with gold leaf, two white sofas faced each other across an immense coffee table, sumptuous drapes kept the city at bay, the lighting was subdued and indirect, casting shadows and highlights across thick carpet, polished wood, gilt-framed artwork.

Roddy McDowell sat on one sofa, his legs tucked up under him, a cocktail in his hand. There was a very thin man in an expensive suit standing behind an armchair, holding the leash of the ocelot that sat in the chair. There was a large older woman with a puffy face, bug eyes, thinning apricot hair, wearing a floor-length gold muumuu, sitting on the sofa across from Roddy, smoking and also holding a cocktail.

"Katty-Watkins!" the older woman cried. "Come give your Aunt Didi a huggy-wuggums."

Katrina went and gave Aunt Didi a dutiful hug. The older woman took a deep swallow of her drink. "I've known this kid since she was smaller than a bottle of Beefeater's. Christ, you were an ugly baby. And look at you now—adorable. Just adorable. Christ, I'm proud of you. So fucking proud."

Katrina broke away and headed over to the bar.

"Jean, darling, hand me the phone, I've got to book my flight to Zürich, Elizabeth *needs* me this weekend," Roddy said, before adding in a weary tone, "Dick is acting up."

"Dick Burton is a fucking schmuck. He can kiss my ass," Aunt Didi said.

"Let me call room service, I'll order up a plate of club sandwiches," Jean Clarke said, adding, as if the two were related, "I'm having dinner with Otto Preminger."

"Katrina, darling, you *do* look adorable," Roddy said. Then he turned to me. "Could you get me the phone and freshen my drink—vodka and tonic." He held out his glass.

"I'd be happy to," I said, taking the glass.

"Ah, a gentleman," he said, eyeing me with great significance and then turning away in dismissal.

"Or should I order shrimp cocktails for everyone?" Jean Clarke said.

"The last fucking thing I want is food. Katty-Watkins, you look fucking adorable. Just adorable. You," she said to me, "freshen Aunt Didi's drink while you're up. Scotch with a little water. A very little."

The ocelot was taking it all in with wide green eyes.

"Hi," Katrina said to the man holding the leash. Then she took a long swallow from an enormous glass.

The man, who had a thin haughty face with a big hooked nose, gave a tight-lipped smile.

"The fucking cat belongs to Salvador Dalí," Aunt Didi said. "Spic prick couldn't come himself so he sends a fairy with an ocelot."

I went over to the bar and retrieved ice cubes from the silver bucket.

"Or should I order caviar?" Jean Clarke asked. "Roddy, you love caviar."

I smelled pot and looked over my shoulder—Roddy had lit a joint and was taking a deep toke. "I like *good* caviar, not room-service caviar. Elizabeth better send a car for me or I'm going to spank her."

"Oh please, you goddamn fairy," Aunt Didi said.

I brought them back their drinks.

"Thanks, kiddo," Aunt Didi said.

"Your friend is sweet," Roddy said, offering me the joint; I shook my head. "Sweet but terribly square."

"He looks like another goddamn fairy to me," Aunt Didi said, lighting a cigarette even though she already had one burning in the huge glass ashtray. The ocelot was looking at her in bewilderment.

"Katrina had a Broadway audition today," I said. There was a moment of silence, Katrina bit her lower lip and smiled expectantly.

"Darling, how *wonderful! Bon courage!*" Jean Clarke said, perching on a sofa arm and crossing her lovely legs. "My rehearsals start on Monday, I'm not drinking this afternoon, the *Times* is interviewing me tomorrow, I'm having dinner with Otto tonight. Darling, you *do* look adorable. And you *must* tell us *all* about the audition." Before Katrina could open her mouth, Jean Clarke stood up and moved toward the foyer, following herself in the mirrored wall. "Should I order cheeseburgers for everyone?"

"I knew Katrina when she was knee-high to a bottle of Beefeater's. Ugly kid, you looked like a prune with jaundice. Your father is the biggest bastard in Hollywood, and believe me, I've known them all. Now you're adorable, but why in Christ's fucking sake are you dressed like a boy? Are you a goddamn dyke? Oh shit, that's all I need—a dyke goddaughter."

"I told Elizabeth to sell Gstaad, she can't ski for shit, but ever since she married Dick she's had *grande-dame* syndrome. Deadly affliction. It killed Norma Shearer."

"Should I order hot-fudge sundaes for everyone?" Jean Clarke said, coming back in and taking a cigarette out of a red-glass jar filled with them. She held it up to her mouth and waited, then shot me a glance. I picked up an enormous gold lighter that looked like a pepper grinder, lit her cigarette, and was rewarded with a coquettish smile.

"Hot-fudge sundaes? You trying to make me puke, for Christ's sake?" Aunt Didi said. "That fucking cat is giving me the creeps."

"Katrina goes to school in Connecticut now," Jean Clarke said.

Katrina was petting the ocelot and pretending she was only half listening. Her mother was treating her like a distant relative. It pissed me off.

"Hal Prince was at the audition," I said emphatically. "He's directing the show."

Roddy looked up from his joint and took this in, then said, "If I have to listen to Burton's tired old Dylan Thomas routine one more time, I'm going to kill myself."

"Don't bother, you're already dead," Aunt Didi said.

"Old friends are like fish, after too long they start to smell," Roddy said.

"Fuck you. Katrina, I remember when you were knee-high to a bottle of Beefeater's. Christ, you were an ugly kid. Freshen my drink, will you," she said to me, holding it out, eyeing me with her bug eyes. "What is this, a fairy convention?"

Katrina was over at the bar, drinking straight from the bottle.

"I know, I'll order steak tartare!" Jean Clarke exclaimed, as if that solved everything.

26

KATRINA WAS CALLED back to New York for a follow-up audition and then cast as the lead in the musical, which was now being tailored to her talents. Rehearsals were going to start in the early summer, and the show was going to open out of town in the fall. She was always on the phone, or dashing into Manhattan for a meeting with her agent or Kander and Ebb or Hal Prince or the costume designer or the publicity people. At dinner she would recount the latest developments with great excitement, but it was never quite enough to disguise the fear that I saw in the corners of her eyes. There wasn't a lot of time for school, or for me. I was hurt and jealous, but mostly I was hoping she could handle it all. She was just a kid and there was an awful lot riding on her.

The weather finally changed: crocuses and daffodils opened, pale green buds appeared on hedges and trees, the air had a seductive hint of warmth and smelled of earth and green and promise. I loved spring in Manhattan, but it's a little bit like watching it unfold in a terrarium. Up here in the country, the change was immense, sensual, enfolding, humbling—nature was calling the shots, not Robert Moses.

Spooner was unleashed from the bounds of winter. Mr. Tupper tried to exert control, but he simply didn't inspire—either fear or courage. There was a sense on campus of running out the clock— there was no air left in our tires but somehow we had to keep the jalopy on the road. A lot of the teachers were distracted and anxious, looking for a new job for the fall.

Not Sophia Newcomb. She carried on with her indomitable gravitas, her sad eyes accepting all they saw with wisdom and tenderness.

One balmy morning in April, Discussion class sat in the cabin waiting for her to arrive. Katrina—pale, slack, hung over—was hiding behind a Hermes headscarf and gigantic round sunglasses that almost obscured her face. "I'm *non compos mentis ce matin*," she whispered to me. Sapphire, free and loose in a low-cut peasant blouse, had told me at breakfast that Katrina had arrived back from Manhattan in a limousine at three in the morning. Nicholas was sullen and his fingernails were dirty. Lenny was sitting next to me, bouncing his leg against mine. At one point he grabbed my hand under the table and pressed it against his crotch. I tried to pull away but he held it there and started to hump. Men.

Sophia Newcomb walked in carrying an armful of old plaid blankets, the kind that make you think of summer nights by the sea.

"It is too glorious to be inside. Come, children."

She led us across the field, and we laid out the blankets under the spreading, budding limbs of an enormous old oak. Sophia—wearing a full black skirt and red shirt, her thick black hair piled atop her

head and stuck through with a tortoiseshell comb—gestured for all
of us to sit in a circle. When we had settled, she closed her eyes and
drew in a deep breath of the spring air. Then she exhaled with a sigh,
opened her enormous soulful eyes and looked at each of us in turn.

"There is much to discuss," she said. "It is in the air—a *shift*.
Movement. Transformation."

"Spring!" a Volvo girl in a long flowered dress cried. Then she
smiled with faux-modesty, as if she had just uttered something
wildly original.

Sophia Newcomb considered this. Then she uttered ". . . spring
. . ." in a voice that made it sound closer to nuclear winter.

"Spring is a fucking cliché," Nicholas said.

"Spring might be a cliché," a Volvo boy said, "but cynicism is a
dead end."

"*Life* is a dead end, sweetheart."

"Spring makes me horny," Sapphire said.

"Waking up makes you horny," Nicholas said with a snort.

"So does going to sleep," Sapphire said—and Nicholas smiled for
the first time in a week.

"I really have just *had* it with you, Sapphire," the Volvo girl cried,
"you and your whole stupid stuck-up crowd, you're awful and vulgar and you cheapen everything! You ruined this school with your
drugs and your . . . your . . . *grooviness*. I could have gone to Thatcher
or Putney, they're real schools, and now I won't even have an alma
mater! It's not fair! I HATE YOU!"

Volvo girl leaped up, bawling, and ran—dress and hair flying—
up the hill to the girls' dorm.

There was a long silence. Did I see the tiniest smile flicker at the
edges of Sophia's mouth?

"Spring brings forth much . . . emotion," she said.

"And much assholeism," Sapphire said, her own face melting into tears. "Mr. Tupper is the one who killed our school, there are drugs at every school, but he had to go call the police, it wasn't our fault, we loved it here, we loved it . . ." Tear-streaked and quivering, she looked about four years old, like a tyke who'd skinned her knee.

Katrina put her arms around Sapphire and kissed her face again and again.

Just then two station wagons came into view and stopped at the end of the field. An elderly man got out of the passenger side of the first car. He was quite effeminate, wearing white linen slacks, a white tunic top, and an enormous straw hat. He looked around the campus with wide searching eyes. A crew of much younger men and women got out of both wagons, the backs of which were packed with equipment of some sort.

"Oh shit!" Katrina exclaimed. "That's Cecil Beaton—he's here to photograph me for *Vogue*, I completely forgot." She reached into her bag, took out a pill bottle, shook one into her palm, and swallowed it down dry. "Mother's little helper . . . Cecil, darling, we're over here!" She waved in his direction.

Cecil smiled and headed our way. He had a vague, deliberate walk that conveyed an airy glamour. Katrina jumped up to greet him, pulling me up with her. "There you are, dear girl, *hiding*," he said in a *veddy* upper-crust British accent.

"Oh, Cecil, you scamp," Katrina said. She pulled me in close and lowered her voice. "Cecil Beaton, this is Arthur MacDougal. Arthur is my best friend in the world, he's terribly clever and kind and talented, and I just think the two of you should know each other."

Cecil and I shook hands. "How do you do?" I said.

"I'm delighted to meet you, Arthur," Cecil said, tilting his head and batting his eyes. Then he looked around. "Isn't this wonderfully

Connecticut?" He gestured to the lake. "It's perfect, but we must find a rowboat." He turned and called to one of his crew, "Owen, do find me a rowboat." Owen, young and handsome, nodded and hastened off in search of one. "Do you know, dear girl, that you are the talk of the town, the talk of *both* the towns—you're *it*. Suddenly Twiggy is yesterday."

"But I love Twiggy!" Katrina said. Then she turned to the rest of the class. "Cecil, these are my friends, and our wonderful teacher, Sophia Newcomb. Everybody, this is Cecil Beaton, who is the *most* marvelous photographer."

I could see the pill kicking in as Katrina slipped into her show-biz persona—warmth, charm, dash, wit. It was almost as if she was playing her mother playing Katrina.

Cecil gave everyone a *noblesse oblige* smile. "What a pleasure."

"Good morning, Mr. Cecil Beaton," Sophia said, with a little *noblesse oblige* of her own. Cecil gave her a second look.

I sat back on the ground. There was a lot of activity around the station wagons as camera equipment and clothes were unloaded.

Just then Mr. Tupper burst out of the main house and strode over to us. He looked harried, and was wearing high-waisted polyester slacks, a short-sleeved shirt with a plastic pen-protector, and rubber-soled shoes.

"Just what is going on here?" he demanded.

Cecil looked at him, mildly aghast.

"Mr. Tupper, this is Cecil Beaton, he's here to take my photograph for *Vogue*," Katrina explained.

Mr. Tupper struggled to take all this in; clearly he'd never heard of Cecil Beaton. "Yes, well, Beaton, this is a school." He gestured to all the activity around the station wagons. "This disruption is unacceptable."

sebastian stuart

Cecil stood there, dripping *sang-froid*.

Owen ran up. "There's no rowboat on campus. I'm going to go into town and find one."

"Wood, old," Cecil directed.

Owen flew off on his mission. A young woman appeared holding two chic little evening dresses on hangers—she held them up for Cecil.

"Steam them both," he said.

"Whom do I see about setting up a makeup and wardrobe room?" the woman asked.

"You may use that cabin there," Sophia said, pointing to her classroom. She was taking everything in with bemused equanimity, giving us meaningful looks, as if there was much to learn from what was unfolding.

"Just a minute here. Not so fast. You can't just appear on campus and take over. There are procedures for this sort of thing. I should have been consulted. Official permission needs to be granted," Mr. Tupper said.

There was an appalled pause. Sophia Newcomb rose from the ground.

"Mr. Tupper, I'm afraid I'm the one who must be lashed. I gave Katrina permission," she said.

Mr. Tupper puffed out his cheeks and exhaled in a burst. "Well, *I'm* the headmaster of this school, and I did *not* give permission. I think we have to convene a meeting in my office to discuss this."

Just then Volvo girl reappeared, walking sprightly, her hair freshly combed, mascara on her lashes.

"Hello, Mr. Beaton, I'm Clare Wilton. My cousin is an attaché to the ambassador to the Court of St. James." Then she curtsied.

"Is he?" Cecil said.

Katrina turned to us, lifted her sunglasses, and crossed her eyes. Lenny laughed and threw his arm over my shoulder.

Behind them, the crew was busy moving their stuff into the cabin.

Volvo girl turned to Mr. Tupper and lowered her voice. "Cecil Beaton is the official photographer of the British Royal Family. *So cool it!*"

Mr. Tupper took a step backwards.

Volvo girl turned back to Cecil. "Katrina and I are classmates, dorm mates, and . . . soul mates."

A thin, pretty young man with masses of brunette hair appeared from the entourage.

"Hi, Katrina, I'm Way Bandy, I'm going to be doing your make-up," he said in a soft voice with a Southern accent.

"I know you, darling Way," Katrina said. "And boy do I need you today." She lifted her sunglasses and presented her face.

Way swooned. "That face."

"That sunk a thousand ships," Katrina said.

"Speaking of which, where's my rowboat?" Cecil asked.

"I would like to convene a meeting," Mr. Tupper said. Everyone ignored him.

"Cecil, could you be an utter love and take of a few snaps of me with my chums?" Katrina said.

"Of course, dear child. Then I want you in a tiny elegant little dress, in a battered rowboat, on the high seas of deepest Connecticut."

Katrina jumped up and down, clapping her hands with joy.

Cecil gestured and an assistant appeared with a camera on a tripod.

"I would like to get you as I found you—surrounding your charming and formidable professor," Cecil said with a gracious smile at

Sophia. Everyone got back into their pre-Cecil positions and he appraised the tableau through the camera. "Too many children around the edges, it's muddy, no focus. Cut, edit."

"Oh, Cecil, you do have the sharpest eye. Let's just have my dearest amigos in the picture," Katrina said, pulling Sapphire, Nicholas, Lenny, and me in close.

Volvo girl tried to edge her way in, but Cecil said to her, "I'm sorry, but could you please move away?"

She got up with a quivering smile.

"The Royal Family, huh?" Mr. Tupper said to her. She ignored him, and hovered around in a proprietary way.

Owen returned from town with an old wooden rowboat sticking out of the back of the station wagon. "Bravo," Cecil called.

Katrina took off her headscarf and her sunglasses. Way Bandy worked on her face for about thirty seconds—powder, lips, eyes. Another young man appeared and worked on her hair for another thirty. The transformation was striking—suddenly she was all round eyes and spiky black hair, the sublime waif, gamine and knowing.

"Now, as you were, please. Sophia, you teach. Children, you learn," Cecil said.

Katrina gave us a smile of encouragement, and then turned her focus to Sophia, ready to hang on every word. She was remarkable to watch: natural and artificial, relaxed and tense, above all charming and compelling.

Sophia marshaled her infinite wisdom, and began:

> *Twinkle, twinkle, little bat*
> *How I wonder what you're at*
> *Up above the world you fly*
> *Like a tea tray in the sky.*

She worked her way through most of the verse from *Alice in Wonderland* as Cecil Beaton snapped away. By the time he was done, most of the school had gathered around, and Mr. Tupper had put himself in charge of crowd control, asking everyone to stand back and keep their voices down—the British Royal Family's official photographer was at work.

27

IT WAS A couple of weeks later, a Saturday, and I was down by the lake, alone, indulging in my newest hobby, cuticle chewing. I still hadn't heard from colleges. What if none of them accepted me? Could I work at the Regency full-time, forever? Work my way up to manager? Or maybe I should do the youth-hostel-in-Europe thing. Isn't that what kids my age did to "find" themselves? It was a nice day, but the campus felt deserted—Nicholas had disappeared into the city for the weekend, Katrina had just gotten back from the city, Sapphire was off with Ernie, her black lover from Trinculo. Katrina's magic wheel was turning ever faster. There were all sorts of write-ups and mentions of her in newspapers and magazines. They all stressed that she wasn't riding on her family name, or her looks—this kid had talent to burn. That's what was so upsetting—she *was* burning it, with all the late nights, the champagne, the pills. I picked up a rock and tried to skip it across the water. It sank straight to the bottom.

I heard a car door slam out on the road and then, "Thanks for the ride."

I turned and saw a boy looking up at the Spooner School sign and then down the drive. He was tall, tan, lanky, with long dirty-blond hair pulled back in a ponytail, and had a dog, a black and white mutt, on a rope leash. He saw me and smiled. I smiled back.

"Come on, Garcia," he said, coming toward me. He was carrying a backpack and wearing faded jeans slung low on his hips, a plaid shirt, jean jacket, and high-top sneakers.

"Hi," I said.

"Hi."

Up close he had a beautiful open face with smooth skin, a strong jaw, a few days of hopeful beard, and wide blue eyes with dark circles of fatigue under them; he didn't seem at all conceited about his beauty, in fact his manner was shy, if determined.

Garcia leaped up against me, I leaned down to pet him and was rewarded with wet sloppy affection—the dog's kisses felt warm and comforting. I looked up at the boy and noticed a hearing aid in his left ear. I found the sight of it touching, and a little sexy.

"He's a good dog," the boy said.

"He sure is." Garcia was crazed with excitement, his whole body wagging. "By the way, my name is Arthur."

"Hi, Arthur, I'm Curtis." He held his hand up and for a second I was confused, then realized it was the hippie shake. We shook and he smiled, a guileless smile. "This is the Spooner School, right?" I nodded, and he sighed with satisfaction. "Good. This is what I'm looking for. Boy, am I tired." He slipped off his pack, lay down on the grass, and closed his eyes. "We've been on the road for four days."

"Where did you come from?"

"California. Me and Garcia hitched from Huntington Beach."

"You hitchhiked all the way? Wow. Was it hard?"

"Nah. Got picked up by a couple of weirdos, but that's cool. Weirdos are people, too." He propped up on an elbow and looked around. "Boy, it sure is pretty here."

"You've never been East before?"

"I've never been out of California. Say, you ever swim in that lake?"

"I did once."

Garcia was straining at the leash, frantic with curiosity and joy.

"Maybe you should let him run free a minute," I said.

"Good idea." He untied the dog and it bolted around, smelling wildly, hitting pay dirt, rolling over, waggling on its back. "I love animals. That's all I need: Garcia, the ocean, and Katrina."

"Katrina?" I asked, startled.

"Yup. Katrina Felt. She goes to school here, doesn't she?"

"She does, yes." My mind was racing—could this be the "inappropriate" boy Katrina had alluded to way back in September?

"That's why I'm here, to see her."

"Oh."

"Do you know where she is?"

"Um, she's probably in the girls' dorm, it's that building up on top of the hill over there."

Curtis looked up at the dorm—he bit his lower lip, his California nonchalance replaced by insecurity and doubt. He sat up, cross-legged, and picked at the grass. "I haven't seen her since last summer."

"So you and Katrina were friends out there?"

"More than friends."

"Oh." I was dying for details but sensed I should wait, let him take the lead.

We sat in silence for a little while, watching the ecstasies of Garcia, who plunged into the lake and splashed about.

"You seem like a nice guy, Arthur."

"Thanks, so do you."

Curtis took rolling papers and a pouch of tobacco out of his backpack. He methodically rolled a perfect cigarette, which he offered to me.

"No, thanks."

He lit the cigarette and took a few puffs. Then he left it in his mouth as he released his ponytail from its band, shook out his hair, gathered it back up, and put the band back on. These rituals seemed to restore some of his confidence.

"I want Katrina to come back with me. I have a job now," he said, a hint of defiance in his voice. "I don't spend all my time at the beach. I'm a veterinary assistant. I have my own apartment. We can start over. I'm eighteen now, she's almost eighteen. Her parents can't stop her, they can't stop *us*. Not this time."

Garcia bounded out of the lake and shook himself off, spraying us with water. He ran over to Curtis, bumped him with wild gratitude, then flipped over and presented his belly. Curtis scratched his tummy and Garcia went still, into a canine coma of bliss.

"So you think Katrina's up in the dorm now?" Curtis asked.

"Probably."

"Well, this is what I came for, guess I'll head up there."

"Want me to walk you?" I said, both burning with curiosity and thinking that Katrina might want me there as a buffer, an emotional shock absorber.

"Hey, thanks, man." We set off, Garcia racing ahead. "So, are you and Katrina good friends?"

"Yes. I love her, she's amazing."

He stopped walking and looked at me. "You love her?"

"I'm gay, Curtis."

He laughed. "That's cool, dude." We walked on. "She *is* amazing, isn't she? We had so much fun together. Till it all got freaky."

"Freaky?"

"With Emily." He sighed and kicked at the ground.

"Who's Emily?"

"Katrina didn't tell you about Emily?"

"No."

"That's weird. And you two are tight?"

I nodded.

"Emily was our baby, man."

Garcia ran and took a flying leap at Curtis, nearly knocking him over. Then he took off again.

"Katrina had a baby?" I managed.

"Yeah. Last summer."

Suddenly the sun was too bright, bouncing off the leaves and gravel. I felt dazed, wanted to sit, somewhere cool and shady.

"Hey, you okay, Arthur? You look pale."

"No, I'm okay."

"I was there when she was born, they couldn't stop me. We only had her for twenty-four hours, in the hospital, one day, but we both fell in love with her." His tender tone turned bitter. "Then they took her away. It was mostly her father—man, is that dude harsh. She was *our* baby."

"But I thought Katrina was in school in Switzerland last year."

"They sent her to Switzerland after Christmas, to get her away from me. She was already pregnant but they didn't know it," he said, slowing down, kicking at the ground, thoughtful. "She didn't tell anyone at that fancy-ass Swiss school. Then when she couldn't hide it anymore they sent her home. Boy, was that a mistake. I don't know where her mom was, but her dad flipped out bad. I mean *really flipped.* He'd call me up and just scream and scream, that I was trash, not good enough for his daughter." He looked at me in dismay, reliving it. "And he tried to force her to, you know, have an operation to get rid of the baby, but it was too late. He got his lawyers to get a restraining order against me. Like I was dangerous or something. I don't even like to kill insects. The whole thing messed Katrina's head up so bad. She tried to kill herself."

Garcia was running crazed circles around us. We were on the hill, approaching the girls' dorm. How could Katrina not have told me all this? I suddenly felt as if I didn't know her at all, as if the person she had been with me was just a character she was playing. I felt hurt, angry, at sea.

"But I have a job now, I make decent money and I'll get a raise every six months. I don't spend all day surfing anymore. Are you sure you're okay?"

I nodded. "You better put Garcia back on the leash before we go in."

"Good idea."

The sounds of Bobby Darin singing *Mack the Knife* came from behind the door of Katrina's room. I knocked.

"Come in," she called.

She was sitting on the floor painting her toenails, a drink beside her. Charlotte was asleep on the bed. Katrina looked up at Curtis and Garcia and for a second shock swept over her. Then she leaped up. "Curtis! Baby!" She threw her arms around his neck and hugged

him tight. Garcia went nuts, jumping up onto Katrina. Charlotte
woke up, saw the dog, arched her back and hissed. "Oh, Curtis and
Garcia, my babies, my beautiful babies!"

Curtis was grinning from ear to ear. Then they kissed, hard and
deep. They kept kissing. I felt ridiculous standing there, as yet another
facet of Katrina was revealed—a California beach kid, a chick who
could fall for a dude like Curtis. Finally she turned and looked at me,
her eyes filled with tears—and they weren't tears of happiness.

"Oh, Artie, sweet boy, would you leave us alone for a little
while?"

28

I WAS PULLED from sleep by a hand on my forehead, smoothing my hair, gently, tenderly. I opened my eyes.

"Good morning, Artie," Katrina said with a sweet, soft smile. She was sitting on the edge of my bed, looking drawn and exhausted but trying not to show it.

"What time is it?"

"It's early."

The light coming in the window was pale and still.

"Did you get any sleep?" I asked.

Katrina shook her head. She smoothed my hair again, touched my cheek, adjusted my covers. "Curtis liked you, he said you were 'solid.'" She laughed a tiny laugh.

"He's a nice guy."

"Isn't he, isn't he a nice guy?"

I sat up and took a good look at Katrina—she looked spooked. "He seems like a great guy."

"He told you about us, about . . ."

I nodded.

Katrina looked down at her hands. "I sent Curtis home, Artie, is that all right?" She looked up at me, beseeching.

I nodded again.

"I had to, you can see that, can't you? Curtis was my old life. I can't go back, you can't go back, you have to keep moving forward, you have to. . ."

"You sent him back to California?"

She nodded. "I got him a plane ticket, a limousine down to the airport, I got a seat for Garcia too. I couldn't stand the thought of that beautiful dog riding with the luggage. Curtis was so sad, it tore my heart up, Artie, he's such a sweet boy, such a kind boy, but I have a new life now, with the play and everything, I can't go back to hanging out at the beach, I can't . . ."

"I understand," I said, even though I wasn't sure I understood anything about Katrina anymore.

"Curtis told you about Emily?"

"He did."

"Don't tell anyone, okay, Sapphire or Nicholas or anyone."

"Okay."

"Please don't hate me for giving up my baby. Please, *please* . . ."

"Katrina, of course I don't hate you, how could you have taken care of her?"

"I could have, I could have gotten help, my parents are rich, I could have done it."

"Katrina, you're just a kid yourself."

"Now I'll never see her again, never, ever, *ever*, she was my baby, my baby . . ."

And then her face slowly dissolved. Her mouth quivered, tears poured down her cheeks, she cried hard, harder and harder, really hard, her face turned red and contorted—I'd never seen anyone cry that hard.

"It's okay, it's okay . . ."

She curled up against me, sobbing, wailing, gurgling, her whole body shaking.

"Katrina, it's okay, really, it's okay."

I pulled the blanket up over her and put my arms around her, but she kept sobbing.

KATRINA FINALLY CRIED herself to sleep in my arms. Her body felt so small and fragile, her rest so tenuous, that I was afraid to move, and so I lay there for hours, wide awake. Outside, it turned into a misty drizzly day. A terrible cosmic sadness came over me as I listened to her gentle breathing. Earlier in the year I had wanted to be her compass, her anchor. I saw now how impossible that was. Her need was so immense it terrified me—I had to keep myself afloat. My arm fell asleep, my legs cramped, and a million jumble-tumble thoughts careened through my exhausted brain, until finally I joined her in sleep.

I was awakened by the smells of chicken broth, vegetables, onions, garlic. I opened my eyes to see Sapphire standing over a one-burner hot plate set on the desk, stirring a large pot.

"Good morning," she whispered.

"Hi," I whispered back.

"Actually it's two in the afternoon."

"Yikes."

"How long has Katrina been asleep?"

"I'm not sure."

"She had a rough night," Sapphire said.

"I know."

"I'm making us a pot of soup, it's a soup day," Sapphire said. "I found this hotplate down in Tupper's old rooms, and I cribbed the ingredients from the kitchen."

Katrina stirred.

"Hi, baby girl," Sapphire said.

I extricated myself from Katrina and sat up. She lay still a minute more and then slowly sat up on the side of the bed, her face smushed, her eyes puffy. She looked as if she didn't know where she was.

Outside it was drizzling and gray, one of those damp chilly Sunday afternoons that make you want to pad around in your socks, eat too many cookies, and avoid doing your homework. Of course, this being Spooner, none of us worried about homework.

"Need to pee," Katrina said, and headed into the bathroom.

"You met Curtis?" I whispered.

"Yes, and he told me."

"Everything?"

"*Everything.*"

"I'm afraid she might try again," I said.

"Me too."

"What should we do?"

"Love her."

Katrina came out of the bathroom.

"Ready for some soup?" Sapphire asked.

Katrina smiled a sleepy smile, sat back down on the bed, and snuggled against me.

Sapphire ladled out of a mug of soup. "Got to keep your strength up," she said, handing the mug to Katrina, who cupped it in both hands and brought it up to her nose.

Sapphire handed me a mug of the soup. It was full of vegetables and chicken and herbs, it tasted like comfort and earth and life. When I was about ten, my family took a vacation in the Dolomite Mountains of northern Italy. One day Ann insisted I hike with her to the top of a mountain. It took hours, and when we got to the top, it was foggy and damp, just like it was today. There was a little house there, and one stout peasant woman who made a living feeding hikers. She was nursing a pot of soup not unlike this one. Ann and I sat on a wooden bench at a wooden table, and she brought us both steaming bowls. I loved my sister that day. And I loved Sapphire today.

"This is so good, Sapphire," I said. "Thank you."

"Eat up, there's plenty more," she said. She ladled herself a mug and sat on Nicholas's bed. Katrina sipped and purred.

"I got a copy of *Wuthering Heights*. Should I read a little aloud?" Sapphire asked.

Katrina nodded.

29

IF APRIL WAS an unfolding, May was an explosion. Suddenly the campus was enveloped in a jazzy sea of green—trees above, grass below, bushes between—translucent green, dark green, and every green in between, all of it swaying, shimmering, softening sharp edges and making the world seem like maybe it was a safe place. One morning I took my breakfast coffee up to the front steps of the boys' dorm and sat enjoying the warm breeze. Morning sun, blue sky, songbirds—it was like a cartoon of happiness. A cartoon was right.

"Arthur, phone," Jeffrey said, popping his head out the dorm door.

What fresh hell is this?

I stepped inside and picked up the receiver. "Arthur?"

"Hi, Mom."

"How are you, darling?"

"Fine."

"No need to bite my head off. Are things on an even keel up there?"

"Yes."

"You got a letter. From San Francisco State College. Shall I open it?"

I could tell she already had. "Yes."

"You've been accepted."

"Oh," I said, surprised that any college would take me.

"Well, you don't sound too thrilled."

As the news sunk in, I felt an ember of excitement. "I'm happy."

I heard her light a cigarette. "Do you think you'll go?"

"Yes."

"It's awfully far away."

"Well, Mom, it was the only school that accepted me, so it's either San Francisco State or nothing."

"I'm sure it's a very good school."

"How are you and Dad?"

"We're fine. Your father is very proud of you. We both are." She sounded as if she meant it, and it felt nice to hear.

"Thank you, for everything."

"It won't be long till graduation, will it?"

"Less than a month."

"Goodness. I remember your first day at the Grace Church School," Mom said wistfully. "Do you remember Miss North, your kindergarten teacher?"

"Not really."

"She was all bones and smiles. She adored you. You brought home a finger painting that first day and told us it was a giraffe. And now . . ."

Mom almost never got sentimental, so when she did it was particularly embarrassing.

"How's Ann?" I asked, knowing that would snap her out of it.

"She's off to Senegal in June, to teach irrigation. I mean, she can't even thread a needle. But isn't that marvelous, we're terribly proud of her, too."

I wanted to get off the phone, to savor and share my news. "It's a beautiful day."

"Isn't it? Central Park is abloom."

"Good-bye, Mom."

"Good-bye, darling. Congratulations."

I stood there a moment, looking out the screen door at the green day, knowing my life had just changed. San Francisco! I had a wildly romantic image of the place: the Barbary Coast, *The Maltese Falcon*, *Vertigo*, gay mecca, fog, hills, hippies—my future.

I went into my room, sat on Nicholas's bed, and shook him awake.

"Nicholas, I was accepted at San Francisco State!"

"Calm down, man, they accept chimpanzees," he said, even though he still looked asleep.

"Good, I like chimps."

He sat up and lit a cigarette. "So, San Francisco."

"Yup," I said.

"That's terrific, Arthur." He looked sad for a moment. "It's a great town, it's gorgeous, and, you know, there's a lot happening."

"When are you going to hear from Harvard?" Although he kept quiet about it, Nicholas had very high SAT scores.

"I'm not going to Harvard."

"Nicholas . . ."

"Listen, I'm very happy for you, now let's drop all this college bullshit. It's a million years away anyway."

I headed up to the girls' dorm to see how Katrina was doing
and tell her my news. The door to her room was closed and I
hesitated, dreading what kind of shape she'd be in. Since Curtis's
visit, she'd developed a taste for tranquilizers and was spending
a lot of time sleeping—in between trips to New York and occa-
sional appearances in class. There was an open door across the
hall and I went in—the room was unoccupied, late morning light
was streaming through lime polyester curtains, giving the room
a sickly hue.

"Hi there, cutie pie." Katrina was in the doorway, looking fresh
and showered in khakis, a sweatshirt, and fluffy-lined moccasins; she
was carrying a book.

"Hi, Katrina," I said, disguising my surprise.

She walked in, a bounce in her step, and sat on the edge of the
bed opposite me. She gave me a bright beatific smile, but her eyes
were shining and she spoke very fast. I guess she had switched back
to the uppers. "I'm reading the most remarkable book." She held it
up. "*The Fire Next Time* by James Baldwin. It's all about the civil rights
struggle and how black people have been treated in this country. It's
terribly moving and awfully important. It's definitely a book that
would have had an enormous influence on Becky."

"Becky?"

"Becky Webster, the girl I'm playing. Not playing—*becoming*. I've
signed up for private acting lessons with Sanford Meisner, he's simply brilliant, *everyone* has studied with him—Kim Stanley, Jessica
Tandy, Geraldine Page. And I'm going to go on some civil rights
marches this summer, because Becky does. They're planning an
awfully big push for the show, I have my own press agent, of course
it will all be about my parents at first, but if that's what it takes.
Everyone says I'm going to be a *big* star. But I don't care about all

that, it's the work that matters. Hal Prince called again. We talk and talk about Becky. She's a very brave girl."

She stood up and looked at herself in the mirror over the dresser, fluffed at her hair.

"I suppose I'll have to put college on the shelf, at least for a year or two, it was a cute idea though, really it was. I have to find an apartment, they're paying me three thousand dollars a week, can you imagine? My *own* money." She gave a little shudder of delight. "Maybe I'll live in Greenwich Village, I think that would be a good image for me, don't you? Sort of a little bohemian. I *have* to be more than Jean Clarke's daughter, everyone agrees on that, develop my own image. My agent says I want to *build* on the foundation of my parents' fame, but not *depend* on it. He's really a very smart man, and so kind and patient, we talk all the time, he makes me feel protected." I felt a stab of jealousy.

Then she looked out the window, then back at herself in the mirror, taking little steps this way and that, never looking me in the eye.

"I better get back to my book. The first script reading is coming up soon, I have to practically start living in the city, but I'm determined to finish out here and get my diploma. Not that I'll really need it. They're sending me to Richard Avedon to be photographed next week, and there are some early interviews lined up." She plopped on the bed beside me, slipped an arm through mine and rested her head on my shoulder. "Oh, Artie, you've been such a wonderful friend." She kissed me on the cheek. "I love you so much." She jumped up. "See you later, Noodles."

And then she was gone.

I sat there in the lifeless, airless room feeling abandoned and insignificant, as if any news of mine couldn't possibly compare to the excitement of Katrina's life. Wasn't friendship supposed to be a two-way street? I felt a stab of anger, but it was quickly overtaken by fear, dread about the direction Katrina was heading, because I knew her well enough to know that I'd just watched a performance—and not a very convincing one.

30

ON A SATURDAY night about a week later, Marcus Lipps, the Andy Warhol acolyte, swept in during dinner. He was well over six feet tall with a striking, sensual face, all sharp angles meeting at a full, pouty mouth, topped by an up-to-the-minute Vidal Sassoon haircut, short in the back with diagonal bangs. Wearing tight bell-bottom jeans and a black turtleneck, he had great presence—and he stood in the doorway making sure everyone knew it.

"Marcus!" Sapphire screamed from the table where she, Nicholas, and I sat.

Marcus took his own sweet time coming over, tossing his head several times, his Vidal Sassoon flying up and then magically falling back to its original shape. Sapphire gave him a hug, which he accepted like

Lana "watch the hair" Turner. He grabbed a chair, turned it around, and sat down cowboy-style, leaning over the back.

"I saw you in *Harper's Bazaar*, superstar, that Factory looks like a first-class freak show," Sapphire said.

"Marcus," Nicholas said with feigned nonchalance.

"This is Arthur," Sapphire said.

Marcus batted his stunning green eyes at me.

"Hi," I said, a bit awed.

"You hungry?" Sapphire asked—Marcus looked like he hadn't eaten in a month.

"Food," he said languidly, as if it was beneath contemplation.

"So, how've you been, man?" Nicholas asked.

Marcus turned to show his profile. "Any *snow*storms this winter?" he said finally.

"Cocaine?!" Sapphire exclaimed. "You have some!"

"Maybe," Marcus drawled.

"Groovy," Sapphire said.

"Groovy is passé."

"Oh, Marcus, get over it, you're back at Spooner, you skinny fag," Sapphire said, attacking his armpit and making him lose his cool in a tickle fit.

"Oh, gimme a bite," he said in exasperation, grabbing Sapphire's plate and wolfing down half her grilled cheese sandwich in one swallow.

⌒

"WHERE'S THIS FAMOUS Katrina?" Marcus asked as he raised the coral coke spoon to his nose.

We were all back at The Spot, sitting in a tight circle, it was a warm spring night, crickets chirped, animals rustled, there was a three-quarter moon rising through the treetops and a soft, fragrant breeze.

"She's in our room, we'll visit her later," Sapphire said.

"I saw her mother at the Brasserie—*very* face-lifted," Marcus said.

He passed around his jade vial and coral spoon. I'd never tried cocaine before and knew I probably shouldn't, but I was in a screw-it-all mood. It burned my nostrils, then a *rush-of-euphoria!*

"This drug is cool," I said, and then wished I hadn't.

Sapphire started drumming her palms on her thighs. "Tell us more about the Factory."

"*Faaa*-bulous . . ." Marcus said, dangling a carrot.

"Well, what do you guys *do?*" Sapphire pressed.

"We don't *do* . . . we *are*. Beautiful people. Happenings. Movies. It's . . . *faaa*-bulous," Marcus said in his maddeningly fractured way.

"Sounds totally pointless," Nicholas said vehemently. "And I don't even like this drug, it hurts my nose and makes me uptight."

"*Makes* you uptight?" Marcus purred.

"No fighting," Sapphire said.

"Who's fighting?" Marcus said, eyes wide in mock shock.

"I am," Nicholas said, "Marcus is cruel and shallow."

Marcus flicked his hair. "Mellow out."

"I'll have plenty of time to mellow out in the grave. You don't even care about Vietnam or civil rights or pollution or anything, Marcus."

"I do so care about politics . . . Lady Bird is a fashion disaster."

Sapphire laughed and this only made Nicholas more furious. "You'd laugh at anything, Sapphire."

"You're probably right."

The coke was giving everything sharp edges, gleaming metallic.

"Asshole," Nicholas said, sounding like he was about to cry.

"You are *not* happening," Marcus said, delivering the ultimate putdown.

"Fuck you," Nicholas said, storming out of the Spot and heading deeper into the woods.

"*Tan*trum," Marcus pronounced.

I jumped up and ran after Nicholas. "Nicky!" The path was narrow, branches brushed against me. "NICKY, WAIT UP!" I lost sight of him. I stopped, surrounded by dark woods—small noises rose up all around me, caws and rustling and peeps, I became disoriented, the woods had swallowed up the path, the treetops blocked out the moonlight, I was lost in branchy blackness, I might never get out, I could freeze to death, what about wild animals, escaped convicts?

"HELP!"

The woods swallowed up my cry. I felt ridiculous. I fought panic. Then I saw a small red ember through the branches: the tip of a cigarette: some lunatic escaped from a mental hospital! He stood there silently smoking, stalking me—and then he made his move.

"Arthur?"

"Hi, Nicky."

"You all right?"

"Fine."

"Did you scream?"

"Me? Scream? No."

"That's weird, I was sure I heard someone scream."

"Probably from back at The Spot. I was looking for you. Are you all right?" I asked.

"That Marcus is such a dick." He was close to me now in the darkness.

"He's very cool."

"He just thinks he is."

"What's with you and Sapphire, Nicholas?"

"When I first came here I was such a mess, I stayed shut up in my room, I was just so bitter. Sapphire took me by the hand and dragged me out of myself. She's so full of life, isn't she? I mean, have you ever seen anyone so full of life?"

"She's pretty great."

"What's going to happen to me, Arthur?"

I had no idea what was going to happen to Nicholas, but his recent reclusive behavior, bitter outbursts, unwashed hair, and dirty clothes all made me very apprehensive.

"You'll be fine," I said.

"Next year I'll be all alone again."

"Did you and Sapphire ever think of doing it?"

"We tried last year one stupid night, she started laughing."

"She loves you, Nicky."

"Yeah. She loves a lot of people. Arthur, I want to marry her and move to the Cape and write and have babies."

"You're seventeen years old."

"So what? It's pathetic, she'll forget all about me by August. Oh, fuck, man, I'm sorry I'm being such a downer. That cocaine freaked me out."

"I did scream before."

"I know."

We laughed.

"So you're not going to go to Harvard?"

"Nah. I'm going to take a year off, hang out in New York City and get into trouble."

"Don't get into too much trouble. And we'll see each other when I come home for visits."

"Yeah."

"Should we head back for the next installment of The Marcus Lipps Show?"

"Why not? Might as well explore my masochistic tendencies."

We set off through the woods.

"You know, you've been a great friend to me this year," I said.

"Really? I thought I was a total prick most of the time."

"Prickly maybe, but never a prick."

"Hey, maybe I'm not totally worthless."

~

NICHOLAS AND I walked into Katrina's room. She was in a chair, keyed tight, trying to sit still as Marcus lined her eyes with a black makeup pencil. Wearing a little black dress, black heels, and a silver bracelet and earrings, she looked wired but stunning, elegant, electric. Sapphire was dancing to Otis Redding and swigging from a bottle of Dom Pérignon. Charlotte was leaping and scampering about.

"We're driving down to the Factory," Marcus said.

"Oh, you must come, Artie, you must-must-*must!*" Katrina gushed.

Sapphire took a swig of champagne. "I'm staying here."

"You are not," Marcus said.

"Ernie, my beautiful black lover, is coming over."

"Don't you want to meet Andy?" Marcus asked.

"Will Andy fuck me?"

~

MANHATTAN LOOMED LIKE another planet as we crossed the Triborough Bridge. We sped down FDR Drive, and Marcus parked his mom's station wagon somewhere in the East Forties. The night was warm enough for Manhattan to have that acrid sidewalky smell it gets in the summer.

Katrina, Nicholas, and I followed Marcus into a dingy industrial building; the Supremes singing *Baby Love* drifted down the wide stairwell. We climbed three flights, Marcus tossing his hair, raising his chin, growing more fabulous with every step.

The Factory itself was much less glamorous than I'd expected—a large grungy loft, its walls and windows covered with tin foil; thin people were dancing languidly in the middle of the room, others milled about in corners or lounged on ratty armchairs and sofas. Everyone looked restless, like they were waiting for something to happen. I wanted to take it all in, try and enjoy myself, but Katrina was so manic—she kept fluffing her hair and making small jerky motions—that anxiety was just about all I could feel.

Everyone looked at us as we entered and then looked away very quickly—and then looked back at Katrina. Someone rushed up to Marcus and pulled him away.

A small man with a scrunched up, gnomey face, wearing all black and a motorcycle cap covered with slogan buttons and commemorative pins, approached us and smiled, which made him look like the troll who lived under the bridge. He held out his hand—there were white pills in his palm.

"No, thanks," I said.

Nicholas took one, so did Katrina.

"Katrina, don't," I said, but she had already swallowed it. In the center of the room Warhol's most famous superstar, Edie Sedgwick—thin, striking, with short silver-white hair, wearing black tights, high heels, and a T-shirt—was dancing with herself; she shot Katrina a glance.

"Edie *is* the sixties," the little man said.

Then he moved very close to me. Nicholas took Katrina's hand and started to lead her away.

"Where are you going?" I asked them.

"Just to get something to drink. Mellow out, man," Nicholas said.

"We'll be right back, darling," Katrina said as they wandered off.

"I'm famous. I want to suck your cock," the little man said, his face next to mine; his breath smelled like Sen-Sen, he stared into my eyes.

"Thanks, but I don't think so."

"I have a house in the Pines, I'm very rich. What are your favorite drugs?" Suddenly he turned away. "Andy. Fabulous night. Zefferelli is here. Naomi Sims. Norman Mailer is coming. Jimi Hendrix is at the Regency. We *must* get him over."

"Hi," Andy Warhol said to me in a high, breathy voice.

It was shocking and exciting to have his famous pasty face in front of me, but it wasn't enough to overcome my anxiety.

"Hi," I answered. Andy stood staring at me. He leaned in and whispered something to the little man, then he giggled.

"Is that Katrina Felt?" the little man asked, pointing to Katrina.

"Yes."

Andy and the little man exchanged glances.

"She's fabulous beyond fabulous," the little man said.

"She's having a hard time," I said.

"She's going to own the world."

"I don't think that's what she wants."

Andy looked at the little man.

"Bring her over," the little man said.

I hesitated.

"Please," Andy said with a shy smile, followed by a little giggle.

Katrina and Nicholas were in a small group now—everyone looked languid and tense at the same time. I walked over.

"Katrina, Andy wants to meet you."

Everyone watched as we walked away. Katrina's body was vibrating, almost as if she had the chills; she was smiling this huge, strained smile.

"Hi," Andy said to Katrina.

Katrina just kept smiling.

"You have *it*," the little man said. "You're Jean Clarke's daughter. That's fabulous. We had dinner together in Positano. But your look is much more *now*. I'm taking you over to Eileen Ford myself."

Everyone in the room kept looking at us. Edie was dancing harder.

Andy and the little man exchanged a glance.

"Andy's making a movie tonight, he wants you in it, come on," the little man said. He took Katrina's hand and he and Andy began to lead her away from me.

"Katrina, are you sure you're okay?"

"Di*vine*, darling," she said—and then she shuddered.

Andy turned and gave me a little wave. They walked to the other end of the loft, where a thin young man was filming another thin young man's foot.

I felt a little queasy and sat on a window ledge near the door, to make sure Katrina didn't leave without me. A fat girl in a very short dress appeared, her frizzy red hair sticking out all over her head.

"Isn't this *fabulous* I mean don't you just *love* Andy he's a *genius* I'm a stylist I work with *Halston* he's fabulous so *now* I was in London last week London is *very* now I worked with *Avedon* yesterday he's *fabulous* so fast knows *exactly* what he wants— so *now*! My name is Wallis

isn't that *fabulous* I was at Max's and I said '*I-want-a-new-name!*' and
Andy just said 'Wallis' I was *named* by Andy Warhol I was at *Halston's*
and *Liza* said, 'Esther, roll another joint' and I said 'Liza, I'm *Wallis*
now—*Andy* named me' Liza said that was *so* now so totally *of the
minute*. I'm speeding."

I never would have guessed.

Wallis walked away.

I went looking for Katrina. I saw her at the center of a clutch
of people—they were hovering, she was shaking. I pushed my way
through.

"Please get me out of here," she whispered.

"Have you seen Nicholas?"

"No, but I *have* to get out of here, Artie, please."

"Come on, let's just take a quick look for him," I said, taking her
hand. Everyone watched as we walked away. Edie was still dancing.

In the back of the loft we passed a sofa with a naked girl on it—
she had shaved eyebrows and an overbite, was holding an empty
Coke bottle in her hands. A small group of people stood around,
urging her to put the Coke bottle inside herself. We turned a corner and were in a small kitchen alcove. Nicholas was sitting at the
kitchen table; the sleeve of his J. Press shirt was rolled up, a belt
tied around his bicep. A young man in a black T-shirt was crouched
on the floor in front of him, slapping the inside of his elbow; long,
sinewy veins snaked down the length of Nicholas's arm—the young
man inserted a hypodermic needle into one. I watched with fasci-
nation and horror as blood flowed from Nicholas into the needle,
mixing with its milky contents—then the young man pumped the
mixture back into Nicholas. His eyes opened very wide and then
closed half way. His face relaxed. He looked up at me. His eyes were
shining. He smiled.

"Nicholas, we're leaving," I said. "Don't you want to come with us? Please, come on, let's get out of here."

He smiled again.

Katrina pulled on my hand, frantic, and we bolted out of the Factory.

We grabbed a cab.

"Sherry-Netherland," I told the driver.

Katrina curled up on the back seat, her body trembling, her face glistening, her eyes wide, unfocused. "What's happening to me?"

I had no idea but I knew it was bad, really bad. I felt sweat break out on my forehead, my throat constricted. "Do you want to go to an emergency room?"

She shook her head in panic and slunk even further into herself. I was trying to think, without much success, and just hoped that she would calm down when we got to the safety of her mom's apartment.

We dashed through the hotel lobby, past a shocked phalanx of doormen and porters, and into the elevator. Jean Clarke's apartment was dark and empty. I led Katrina into the living room and turned on a few lights.

"Why don't we just sit down and try to relax," I said, sitting, sucking air, trying to set an example.

"I'll be right back." She disappeared.

There was a lanky Giacometti sculpture of a man on the coffee table. I picked it up—he looked almost as spooked as I was. I waited. No Katrina. I got up and went to one of the four large windows that looked out over Central Park. My folks' apartment was just two blocks away, but I felt like I was hurtling away from them, into another world.

"Katrina?"

The apartment absorbed my voice in an instant, just swallowed it up. There was no answer.

I moved into the foyer.

"Katrina?"

Just then the front door opened and Jean Clarke walked in. She was startled for a moment, but recovered in a snap. "Why, hello," she said in a warm low voice.

"Oh, hello, Miss Clarke."

She was wearing a short metallic gold dress that picked up light and made her glitter; her glittery hair was teased up over her forehead and then swept down to frame her face.

"Um, Miss Clarke, Katrina is, ah, having some problems."

Her smile faded, replaced with a look of concern. "What sort of problems?"

"I'm not sure, but, um, I think they're serious, the thing is we came in and now I don't know where she is."

"You don't know where she is *in the apartment?*"

"Yes."

"Well, I'm sure we can find her. Have you looked in the bedrooms?"

"No."

Jean Clarke swept by me and I thought I detected a look of annoyance on her face. I followed her down a hallway. She walked into a bedroom and switched on the light.

"Katrina?" she called.

The opulent room was empty, looked like it had always been empty. We checked out the adjoining bath. Nothing.

"I wasn't expecting Katrina," Jean Clarke said, glancing at herself in a round mirror that hung over a rococo dresser.

"We came into town with some other students, we were at the Factory."

"Were you? I was there last week, Laurence Harvey took me. Larry adores that whole *scene*. I found it amusing, but a bit much for my taste."

I followed her down the hallway into the master bedroom. It was gigantic and had a bank of windows facing the park—one of them was open and its long white curtains billowed in like dancing ghosts. Had Katrina jumped? Icy fear raced up my spine.

"Where could she be?" Jean Clarke said, standing in the middle of the room with her hands on her hips. "Honestly."

I forced myself to look out the window—it was a long way down. But there was no sign of a body, no commotion.

I turned—Jean Clarke was standing stock still in front of an open closet, her mouth open.

"What is it?" I asked.

She didn't answer.

I walked over to her and looked in the closet. It was a walk-in, enormous, with deep wooden shelves. I swept my eyes along the rows of clothes and shoes. Nothing. Then I looked up—on the top shelf, over in the far corner, curled in on herself, quivering, was Katrina. In the dim light I could just make out her eyes, huge, round, stark with terror.

"Katrina!" I cried.

Jean Clarke still didn't move, but I could see her shock fade and her thinking begin.

"I have to call my lawyer," she said, moving toward the phone.

31

I WAS EXPECTING something a little more imposing—after all, it was the toniest mental hospital in Manhattan—but the building was disappointing, boxy fifties-modern, brick, sort of like a suburban high school built vertically. It was early evening and hot, that awful New York City hot, dirty, sticky, and claustrophobic, and the air conditioning hit me like a blast from the heavens. It was two weeks after that terrifying night. In the afternoon, after class, without a word to anyone, I'd walked out to the road and flagged down the bus to the city.

I kept my guest pass highly visible as I waited for the elevator; I didn't want anyone to mistake my status.

The elevator opened onto a wide hallway, empty except for one teenage girl with stringy hair wearing slippers and crying.

An older nurse appeared. "May I help you?"

"I want to see Katrina Felt."

"Room Nine."

I peeked into rooms as I passed: they were all identical, two beds neatly made up with brightly colored bedspreads, two dressers, two chairs. That was about it. One had a porcelain doll on the dresser, but mostly they seemed eerily lifeless.

The door to Room Nine was closed. An immaculate middle-aged nurse materialized and opened it. "Closed doors are not allowed," she said with an efficient smile. Then she disappeared.

Katrina was sitting in one of the hard little chairs, her hands folded in her lap.

"Hi, Katrina."

All the life was gone from her face, it looked numb, as if she had seen something so unspeakable that it froze her face. She looked up at me and a faint smile cracked the mask. "Hi, Arthur." Her voice was slow and flat; they definitely had her heavily medicated.

I flashed on our first meeting, on the front steps at Spooner back in September, how buoyant and feisty and funny she'd been, her face so expressive, so full of stories to tell, adventures to come.

"How are you feeling?"

"I'm okay," she said. She looked down at her hands.

I wasn't sure how I should behave, I wanted to try and cheer her up but I didn't want to be all hale and hearty. "I brought you a present." Her expression didn't change. I took out the large picture book on the Brontës' Yorkshire I'd just paid thirty-five dollars for at Brentano's. "Look, here's Haworth Parsonage," I said, holding it open. "This is Charlotte's room. And look, here's a picture Anne drew of her dog, Keeper. And here's Brontë Falls. Isn't this countryside beautiful?" There was a photograph of a dirt road running

between hedgerows, up a rise, down a dale, off toward a horizon
full of light and promise.

"Oh, Artie, that's beautiful," she said wistfully.

"We should all move there."

Katrina looked down at her hands again.

"Everyone at school misses you, asks after you, sends their love."

"That was a nice school," she said, as if she'd gone there years ago.

"Commencement's next week."

"Oh."

"And Sapphire is taking good care of Charlotte."

"Charlotte."

I got up and looked out the window—the sun was setting, the
neighboring rooftop was a maze of vents and pipes. I wished Katrina
were at some fancy rest home in the country, taking long walks and
eating hearty soups. This place felt all wrong.

Katrina pulled a pack of Marlboros out of her pocket, lit one, and
took a deep drag. "I'm sorry, Artie."

"Sorry for what?"

"For disappointing you."

"Katrina, you didn't disappoint me."

"Yes, I did. You thought I was someone I'm not. Someone funny
and happy . . . with a wonderful future, world's her oyster and
all that. That's who I wanted you to think I was . . . that's who I
wanted to be."

The truth was, she *had* disappointed me, but not because she
wasn't happy-go-lucky all the time; I loved her mercurial moods,
her darkness, her irony. What disappointed me was all the drinking,
taking all those pills, not telling me about Curtis and Emily. I guess
our friendship wasn't enough, not enough to make her happy, to
make her feel safe, to tell me her secrets. I thought I'd made a best

friend and now she was living in a bubble of medication and sorrow, out of reach. But what was the point in telling her all that now?

"You *do* have a wonderful future," I said. "And that *is* who you are. No one can be funny and happy all the time, we're all neurotic and sad and screwy too, but so what, it's all part of the mix. You're strong, Katrina, and brave, and you're going to get past all this, sure you are, kiddo, I *know* you are."

She smiled at me—the saddest smile I had ever seen.

"I'm out of the show," she said.

I wasn't surprised. "There'll be other shows."

A young black attendant walked into the room carrying a huge fan-shaped bouquet that looked like it belonged in the winner's circle at the Kentucky Derby. He put it on the dresser top and stood there, obviously fascinated by Katrina. The bouquet was so big that it dominated the room—it felt like a person. "From your father," the attendant said with a sheepish smile.

"Thank you," Katrina said, and he left. She dropped her cigarette into a glass.

I felt tapped out, drained, I had no idea what I could possibly say or do to help her. None of the room's lights were on and gray Manhattan twilight poured in the window.

"It's evening. Remember, Katrina, the hour between the dog and the wolf?"

She turned and looked at me, and then it happened, a smile, wan but warm, "Our favorite time."

We sat in a nice silence for a while.

Then she reached over and put a hand on my cheek. Her eyes filled with tears and then I couldn't look at her anymore.

32

A DUCK HAD returned to the lake. I had no idea if it was the old duck or a new duck, but I was tossing her bits of waffle I'd saved from breakfast and she was gratefully snapping them up. It was a warm day, but windy, and high clouds skidded across the sky, fleetingly blocking the sun, changing the light. I held out my hand with the last bit of waffle in it; the duck swam closer and stopped, eyed me warily. "It's okay," I told her. She tilted her head slightly in response, then thrust her neck forward and pecked the waffle out of my hand, raised her head, and swallowed it down her long neck. "That's it, my friend." She looked at me for a moment and then turned and swam away.

It was commencement day.

The last weeks of school had been a joke. One morning we were all handed a mimeographed announcement of the Spooner School's permanent closing; it had lost its accreditation from the state of Connecticut and the bank had started foreclosure proceedings on the property. Classes grew spotty at best, the linen service was cancelled, the cleaning man stopped showing up, little piles of debris sprouted in corners.

"Over there we'll put the arts pavilion," I heard Mr. Spooner say. I came around the side of the building to find him and Miss Wimple sitting beside the empty swimming pool, a small table between them set with tea service.

"Oh, Mr. Spooner, what a splendid site!" Miss Wimple gushed as she refreshed his tea.

"I want the building to harmonize with the natural contours of the land. *Harmony*. Such a lovely word."

"My mother had a sister named Harmony. She only lived eight days. Poor Baby Harmony," Miss Wimple said.

"I want to set the science lab back in the woods a little ways, amidst the trees, with glass walls, to bring nature in. Oh, yes, the campus shall be glorious! Why, Arthur, I didn't see you."

"Hello, Mr. Spooner, Miss Wimple."

"Oh, Arthur, how lovely to see you. Congratulations!" Miss Wimple said, dashing over to me and squeezing my hands.

"It's nice to see you both back."

"It's good to be back," Mr. Spooner sighed.

"We've moved into our old rooms," Miss Wimple said firmly.

"There's lots of work to be done," Mr. Spooner added.

"Would you like a biscuit?" Miss Wimple offered, holding out a plate of them.

I shook my head. Hadn't anyone told them that there wasn't going to be a next year; that after today the Spooner School would no longer exist?

"I do hope you'll come back and visit us," Mr. Spooner said, sipping his mad tea.

"Do you remember that rock you had on your desk the first day of school that you showed to me and Katrina, the one that came from the meteor?" Mr. Spooner smiled and nodded. "You told us a story about it, that the Indians had put a curse on it. What sort of curse was it?"

"That wasn't a story about a meteor, Arthur."

"It wasn't?"

"It was about the imagination."

"There was no curse?"

"There was no meteor."

I looked into the empty swimming pool, a vein of grass grew from a crack. I wanted to ask Mr. Spooner why he had made up that story. I was angry at myself for believing it. The sun came out and suddenly the day felt hot and close—an insect buzzed my head.

"I'd better go get dressed," I said.

I had accumulated virtually nothing during the year, so packing was a breeze. No one had seen hide nor hair of Nicholas since that night at the Factory. Sapphire and I had called his house repeatedly; each time the housekeeper told us she hadn't seen him. Sapphire finally reached his father, who brusquely told her that Nicholas had been to his office twice to pick up cash, and that if his son wanted to dig his own grave, so be it. I missed Nicholas terribly, and worried about him, but there was only so much worry I could handle. Sometimes I wondered if the whole year had been a dream and Mom was going to shake me awake and tell me to get dressed for Collegiate.

I was going to start working at the Regency in a week, and I couldn't wait.

I put on a pair of cords, a dress shirt and jacket, and was knotting my tie when Jeffrey appeared in my doorway. He'd grown several inches and filled out during the year, and looked much less cowed by the world.

"San Francisco here you come," he said. "Gay capital of the country."

I smiled. "What about you?"

"I'm going to public school in Stamford." He was wearing a suit and he looked efficient and grown-up somehow; I imagined him a librarian, organized, helpful, reserved but firm.

"Good for you," I said, knowing he'd had to battle his parents not to be sent away.

He looked so proud and serious. He stuck out his hand and I shook it; his grip was strong. "Thanks for being my friend," he said.

"Thanks for being mine."

The handshake felt formal and ridiculous, but right somehow. I suddenly loved him so much.

"You're a great guy, Jeffrey."

His serious face broke into an aw-shucks smile.

"See you later," he said, and left.

I looked out the window and watched the cars arriving. Parents and children got out; there were a lot of spring dresses and straw hats on the women, the men were in light blazers and chinos—for a moment the place almost looked like a real boarding school on commencement day. I saw Mom and Dad pull up and I went down to meet them.

"Congratulations, Arthur," Mr. Tupper said, intercepting me outside the dorm. I waved to Mom and Dad as they headed toward the field, where chairs had been set up.

"Thanks."

"I know we've crossed swords more than once . . ." he began.

"Oh, so what."

He smiled gratefully—like everyone else, he wanted to be loved.

"You going back to Minnesota?" I asked, even though I knew he was.

He nodded. "I've secured a position at a junior college."

"Great."

"You have a lot of potential, young man," he said, patting my shoulder.

I tried to disguise my cringe as a shrug.

"Okay," I said, moving away.

Lenny was leaning against a tree, looking sexy and self-consciously hip in a baggy suit.

"Hey, amigo, you made it," he said.

"Hi, Lenny."

We looked at each other.

"It's over," he said.

"Yeah."

"California dreamin'," he said, and I smiled.

"And you're going to Bard."

"Yup."

I looked down at the grass. I wanted to kiss him. "Lenny?"

"Yeah?"

I looked into his warm green eyes. "I hope you have a great summer."

"I hope you have a great everything." He leaned in and kissed me lightly on the mouth. "To remember me by."

"Oh, I'll remember you."

We walked over to the field together.

"Isn't this exciting," Mom said as I sat next to her. Dad reached over and gave my thigh a squeeze.

As a compromise between the Spooner and Tupper forces,

Dr. Sophia Newcomb was chosen to make remarks and hand out the diplomas. We graduating seniors, all seven of us, had voted to dispense with a valedictorian. A folding table had been set up with a vase of flowers at each end.

Dr. Newcomb was wearing a black dress with a red rose pinned to it; she looked very beautiful. She looked out at us with her mournful eyes. "One journey ends . . . and another begins. I want to say to all the children . . . that life awaits you. *The mystery of your future.* Go forth. Always be kind. That's all I want to say."

At that moment a long black limousine pulled onto campus and all heads turned. It came to a stop and the driver got out and opened the rear door. The model Verushka slunk out, looking eight feet tall in a tiny minidress—she struck a pose, arching her back and putting her hands on top of her head. Esther/Wallis, the fat, frizzy-haired girl I'd met at the Factory, got out and lay on the hood of the limousine smoking a cigarette in a long holder. Then a sexy, dazed-looking blonde boy in suede pants and an open shirt got out and looked around like he had no idea where he was. Finally Nicholas got out. He was wearing tight black pants, black boots, a black shirt with the top button buttoned, and black sunglasses; his hair was greasy, he was unshaven. He walked over and sat in one of the chairs. The rest of his party hung out by the limousine.

I waved to Nicholas, but his sunglasses were so black that I couldn't tell if he didn't see me or just wasn't responding.

"Arthur MacDougal."

I walked up and got my diploma, people were applauding, Sophia Newcomb kissed me.

When the ceremony was over, I went up to Nicholas.

"Hi."

"Arthur," he said, languid.

I wanted to ask him about next year, about this summer, I wanted to talk to him about Katrina, about what he'd been doing, about everything.

"Cool," I said.

We just stood there with nothing to say. It was hard to believe we'd once talked late into the night. Mercifully, Sapphire barreled over, crying like a faucet, Charlotte's head peeking out of her carpetbag. She hugged Nicholas.

"I love you, Nicky."

He smiled a tight smile. "Hey."

"You be careful, Nicky, don't be an asshole."

She turned to me, tears just streaming down her face. I had to turn away—the wind picked up and I noticed something blow off the table.

"It's all right to cry, Arthur."

"I'm fine," I said, petting Charlotte, whom Sapphire's parents were adopting. "And hey, happy trekking." She and a cousin were going to do the Morocco-to-Kathmandu hippie trail.

"Look for my postcards," she said.

We hugged long and hard. Over her shoulder I saw Mom and Dad waiting. I signaled I'd be right there and walked over to the table; lying under it was a rolled up diploma labeled "Katrina Felt." I picked it up and ran to the dorm. I pulled the number out of my wallet and called Katrina's hospital.

"Fifth floor," the crisp voice said.

"May I speak to Katrina Felt, please."

"Hold on."

The dorm was as quiet as the day I'd arrived. The open doors to the empty rooms stretched in front of me, the hallway was that strange mid-day dark, the lonely light of lonely afternoons.

"Hello," Katrina said in a sluggish monotone.

"It's me, Arthur."

"Hi, Arthur," she said in the same flat tone.

I couldn't stop myself, I started to cry. I held the phone away and took a deep breath.

"I have your diploma," I said, fighting to control my voice.

She didn't say anything.

"You're a high school graduate. So am I. Can you believe it?" I said in a rush, wishing I could think of something funny to say.

There was a long silence and I wondered if she was still there.

"Katrina?"

"I'm going back to Switzerland," she said finally.

"You are?"

"To a hospital."

I was relieved, picturing good doctors, mountain air, a chaise longue on a sunny terrace, a chance to maybe sort things out.

"I'll keep your diploma for you . . . Katrina, I'm sorry I didn't do more to help you."

There was another long silence.

"Oh, that's okay. You tried. Silly Artie."

I started to sob.

"Oh, Katrina."

I could hear her breathing. I knew she could hear my swallowed sobs.

"Go out to San Francisco and have a wonderful time, have a wonderful life. That's what I want more than anything, more than anything in the world," she said.

I gulped for air.

"I want *you* to be happy, Katrina."

There was another long pause.

Then she said: "I have to go now."

"Good-bye."

"Bye, Arthur."

I hung up and walked down to my room. I went into the bathroom and splashed cold water on my face over and over again. I opened my suitcase and put the two diplomas in the inside pocket, took some deep breaths, picked up the suitcase, and headed out of the dorm.

"That was a nice, simple ceremony," Mom said as I climbed into the back seat.

"Nice and short," Dad said.

We started down the drive.

I looked over to the stone wall where I'd first clapped eyes on Katrina. And there she was again, walking atop the wall with her arms out, all spiky black hair and enormous eyes, brave and graceful and young.

Oh, that's okay. You tried. Silly Artie.

We passed her and I craned my neck around. That's when she smiled and waved me on my way.

Epilogue

So that was it, the last time I'd spoken to Katrina. From what second- and third-hand information I'd gleaned over the years, she'd never been back to the States, and I've never been back east for more than a brief visit.

I took another look at the painting of Katrina. She *had* come through okay, more than okay, with a palace on the Bosporus, children, an eminent husband, a passionate lover. I had come through okay, too, and I knew Katrina would be as happy for me as I was for her. She had reached out to me that year and pulled me out of myself, shown me how to love. And I loved her still.

I closed the photo album and went into the kitchen to begin dinner: pasta with fresh herbs. I poured myself a glass of wine and found Shirley Horn on my iPod. My much-better half would be home in about a half an hour, and as I chopped the herbs I felt a fierce longing to see him, as if he had been away for weeks or even months, not hours. Evening light was pouring in the kitchen windows, that pearly sad soft San Francisco light that I'd fallen in love with forty years ago and was enraptured with still. It was the hour between the dog and the wolf.

I had recently gotten a rather fat royalty check from a romantic suspense novel I'd written under the ridiculous name of Julia

Malloy St. Claire. I picked up the phone and called the gallery in Edinburgh. It was the middle of the night over there but I left a message asking them to call me first thing: I wanted to buy Mr. Erbani's painting of his fabulous mistress.

Acknowledgments

FOR THEIR SUPPORT and sage advice on this book, I am deeply grateful to my editor, Don Weise, and also to Mitchell Waters, Mameve Medwed, and Chuck Adams. And to Michael Fusco, for the beautiful cover. To Sarah Van Arsdale, for her terrific copyediting. I also want to thank Richard Fumosa, Dale Cunningham, Erica Silverman, Brian DeFiore, and Diane Reverend. And Jonathan Strong, Morgan Mead, and Scott Elledge. And Jemima James, still a jewel.

About the Author

Photo credit: Stephen McCauley

SEBASTIAN STUART HAS written novels, plays, screenplays, and has ghostwritten in every genre imaginable. As a playwright, he was dubbed "the poet laureate of the Lower East Side" by Michael Musto in the *Village Voice*. His first novel, *The Mentor*, was a psychological thriller. *24-Karat Kids*, written with Dr. Judy Goldstein, was published in seven countries. *Charm!* by Kendall Hart was a *New York Times* bestselling tie-in with the soap opera *All My Children*. A native New Yorker, he now lives in Cambridge, Massachusetts with novelist Stephen McCauley. Sebastian has a cabin in the Hudson Valley and his mystery, *To the Manor Dead*, the first in a series set in the region, will be published in June 2010.